With Honor Veiled

By Matt Kirkby

Chapter One

Uzume Tomiko walked along Edo's dusty streets with a delicate grace that belied her wrinkled face and the hints of white in her hair. Her wandering path led through well-known neighbourhoods, past tall and crowded apartment buildings, and into her favourite marketplace, just as the sun was cresting its peak. She wore a pale dress with a hem that draped all the way to the ground, under a cloak of red and blue feathers. Her white-streaked hair was elegantly coiled atop her head in an elaborate style held in place with lacquered sticks. The careful and subtle application of make-up helped to obscure her wrinkled too-red features, though nothing could help to disguise her enormous nose.

No one takes notice of me, Tomiko thought to herself. *The city-dwellers are too simple. They see only the obvious, and seek no deeper meanings.* She fanned her face with a brightly coloured rice-paper fan.

"Clear a path!" a harsh voice called out.

Tomiko felt herself jostled as the crowd slowly parted, clearing the street. "What is this?"

A peddler fell against her and hastily apologized. "I was pushed," he said. "I meant no offence."

"None is taken." Tomiko looked up the street.

Retainers carrying a covered chair were pushing their way through the crowd. Heavily-armed men acting as escorts gave due warning that the chair contained someone important. The crowds, however, parted only reluctantly.

"Probably one of the Tokugawas," the peddler told a friend who was also watching the procession. "The Shogun must keep a watchful eye on his city."

"That he must. And the better to ignore the likes of us."

"Indeed. And thanks to the gods for it." The peddler laughed. "We can live our lives best without closer oversight from the Daimyo."

Tomiko followed the two peddlers towards the market. The covered chair and its bearers were already lost in the throng.

Tomiko nodded to herself in satisfaction.

Townspeople in all their varied sorts thronged the square. Housewives in their casual *hakama*—the wide loose pants had slits down the side for easy movement and were tied at the waist with a sash—hunted for bargains. Prosperous merchants in *kimonos* and embroidered *haori*—wide-sleeved shirts, some tied with a sash, others tucked in, and most open in the front—argued loudly with one another. Ragged farmers fresh from labouring in their rented fields brushed shoulders with fat monks in threadbare robes as they shook their *shakujou* staves—complete with small bells—to announce their approach. Samurai swaggered through the crowds—some dressed in fine *kimonos,* others in *haori* and *hakama*—people parting before them so that each man moved inside a bubble of clear space.

Lowering her head so that no one might notice, Tomiko smiled at the sight of two samurai pausing to glare at one another. *The unadulterated arrogance of some*, she thought. *They think that all must bow to them.* There was always the risk of danger whenever people gathered in such numbers and in such conditions, and Edo *was* known for being a dangerous town. *Not so dangerous as Kyoto, of course,* she thought to herself. *No place can match the tension of where Emperor Go-K?my? Tsuguhito holds court. But then,* she amended, *given that Shogun Tokugawa rules most of Japan from Edo Castle, this city is still constantly in a state of flux.* The city seethed with politics and power plays.

The square was noisy and Tomiko paused, lifting her head to look around in open amusement.

Housewives argued with peddlers. Men haggled with shopkeepers. *Bote-uri* called out the contents of the baskets they carried on their shoulders to tempt shoppers. Children ran freely, darting between the adults. Goats and geese added their own sounds to the market.

Tomiko smiled more broadly. The bustle of the marketplace made her feel alive. *This* was why she had chosen to live in the capitol. This bustle and vibrancy made her feel young even though she had seen far more summers than even she cared to admit. Most of the people in the lower classes lived in very small houses, and a single room in a *naga-ya* apartment building could be the home for a family of seven or eight people. The crowded living conditions encouraged people to spend most of their time away from home and the large public squares in each district were important centres in daily life.

A young man, barely in his twentieth year, brushed past her.

She gave him a look, and then paused to take another longer one.

He had a fine form, tall and slender. He did not seem overly muscular, though his body, seen through the open front of his *haori*, showed the look of one who was no stranger to physical labour. His face and arms were tanned from long exposure to the sun and his dark hair was shaven into a warrior's topknot. He wore a sword at his hip, tucked into a deep red sash that also served to hold up his *hakama*.

The crowd swirled and he was gone.

Pity. Tomiko gave herself a shake. *He's just a boy,* she told herself. With that, she proceeded deeper into the market. *So many nice things on display.* She paused to browse at the stall of a cloth merchant. "Fresh from the countryside?" she asked as she bent over the bolts of silk.

The fat man nodded, a wide smile on his face. "Indeed, Mistress. These bolts have known only the inside of a ship since they were woven."

"A fine weave it is." She rubbed a swatch between her thumb and finger. "I will think on this."

"It would serve as the basis for a lovely *kimono*."

"No doubt it would." She gave him a bow, then turned and walked on.

The cries of peddlers and shopkeepers grew louder.

Tomiko paused long enough to buy half a dozen plums from a *bote-uri*. The peddler had smiled warmly at her and she had noticed that the baskets hanging from his shoulders were filled with ripe fruit. "*Domo arigato.*" She placed the plums into a small sack she had carried with her.

A samurai stalked past, without giving her a second glance.

Tomiko ventured past a small cart from which pale smoke was rising. It smelled quite delicious. "How is the *kinpira-goba*?"

"As fresh as it can be." The old man smiled at her and gestured to the wok resting atop his small fire. "You would like some?"

"Yes. The sun and my stomach both whisper in my ears that it is past lunch."

"One moment then." The peddler filled a small bowl with rice and topped it with some of the braised vegetables from his wok. He eyed the coins Tomiko gave him as eagerly as she eyed the bowl of *kinpira-goba*.

Taking chopsticks, Tomiko hastily spooned the limp vegetables and rice into her mouth. *This is good,* she thought as she ate. *Better than what I have eaten recently at the teahouses.* And probably more appetizing than her own cooking.

Pausing nearby, two women dressed in kimonos complained about the abundance of snakes that plagued their gardens. The peddler watched them. "A sample?" he pressed, but they ignored him.

"The serpents seem especially abundant this summer," the older matron said.

"Indeed. I cannot enjoy my garden without stepping on one or more of the vermin."

"Never have I know it to be so."

"Nor I. Someone should do something."

Tomiko frowned.

"Move along!" the old peddler ordered them in a loud voice. "If you two will not buy my wares, then kindly do not disturb those who have done so by talking of snakes. Be off with you!"

The women sniffed and hurried away.

Tomiko finished her meal and handed the bowl back to the peddler. "It was most delicious," she told him. "*Domo arigato.*"

He bowed to her.

* * *

The late afternoon sun was still above the rooftops when Tomiko retired to the privacy of her *machiya*. Inside her small private home, she stretched out her toes, relieved to at last be able to cast aside the confining shoes. They were most uncomfortable to wear, but the torture was a small price to pay for walking unnoticed among the rest of the city's inhabitants.

With her long and pointed toenails clicking softly on the floor, she minced over to a cabinet and opened the painted doors. She paused a moment, staring at her blurry reflection in the lacquered top.

The face of an old woman peered back at her.

Grimacing, she reached inside and pulled out a silver-chased goblet and a bottle of plum wine.

"Is *this* to be my existence?" she mused aloud.

"There are worse fates."

She turned around, almost dropping the bottle. "Benkei! I have warned you against coming here."

The crow-headed man chuckled softly. He stood in the doorway leading into the back garden. His brown eyes blinked repeatedly and his black feathers ruffled in the breeze. His arms were shaped more like wings than those of a human being, and his back was hunched. He had a stubby tail of green-tipped black feathers as well.

Tomiko ignored his quiet laughter and turned back to the cabinet. She filled her glass with a generous splash of the amber-hued liquid, and then took a sip before turning towards her visitor.

Benkei was still standing in the doorway.

"I would offer you a drink," she told him, "but I know how little you enjoy the taste of plum wine."

Benkei clicked his beak. "Why this foolish obsession with watching over these humans?" He hopped towards her, bird-like, on his claw-tipped feet. "Granted, they are amusing at times, but to live in one of their *cities*?" His teeth-filled beak clacked several times and he rubbed at his ear.

"I am living my life as I choose."

"So you are," he agreed. His black feathers rustled and several on the top of his head lifted in a crest. "The Clans do not understand this."

"Maybe I want more than just what the Clans have to offer," Tomiko told him. She walked away from the cabinet. "Perhaps I want to live a life without the special gifts you and the other *karasu Tengu* take for granted. Maybe—"

"I fear the humans have corrupted you."

"I am willing to take that chance." With that, she turned away from him and paced across the floor towards a small table that held a copper bowl. She struck a flint and watched the sparks fall into the base of a small burner. She carefully sprinkled incense into the flickering flames.

Benkei was clearly unused to being all-but-ignored. He opened his beak, closed it, and then opened it again. His wings flapped, then settled along with his drab *haori*. "The others will not hold your place open forever. Sooner or later, Tomiko-*san*, it will be too late for second chances."

"Perhaps I am willing to risk even that."

A sweet jasmine scent rose from the small burner and wafted through the room.

Benkei laughed again, clacking his beak loudly. "More the fool you then." He tilted his head to the left and studied her with his unblinking eyes. "If you did not exile yourself away from all contact with the Clans, you might have learned something before it is too late."

At that announcement, she turned with puzzlement plain on her face. "Too late? Too late for who?"

Benkei shook his head. "I can tell you no more." He hopped back towards the open door. "I have told you too much already." He stepped into the rear courtyard and pulled the *shoji* screen closed behind him. "Good day."

Tomiko ignored him. He would, no doubt, be gone from her garden long before she could cross the room, let alone open the *shoji* screen. "Let him go and play his games," she muttered crossly. "I am not interested in the games of the Clans. I gave that all up."

She picked up her goblet in her claw-tipped fingers and sipped at the plum wine. It ran across her forked tongue and tickled the back of her throat.

She inhaled the jasmine incense, hoping it would help to calm her.

It wasn't working.

"I need to spend some time in my garden."

Stepping across the room, Tomiko paused briefly before a polished tray that she occasionally used as a mirror. Her wrinkled red face looked back at her with a look of irritation. She brushed a small speck of dust from her enormous nose.

"Life should be lived for one's own happiness." Tomiko opened a small jar and placed several spiced delicacies onto a gold-chased platter. "This is my life, not the one offered by the Clans."

Carrying the tray, she opened the *shoji* screen and stepped into the small courtyard.

She had privacy there, with tall stone walls blocking her garden from the views of anyone in the neighbouring *machiya*. Her townhouse was small, but it was entirely her own and she valued her privacy. *I would not be happy dwelling in one of the apartments.*

The sun warmed the white sand that formed the bulk of her courtyard. Wind chimes tinkled softly from ribbon-wrapped poles. Chrysanthemums bloomed their small gardens and other plants flourished in clay pots.

Benkei, of course, was long gone.

"And good riddance." She popped one of the dried snacks into her mouth.

Chapter Two

The morning breeze was blowing strongly through the open windows. Though still cool, it was bearing hints that it would soon be another warm day.

Tomiko stretched out her arms, trying to regain enough looseness of limb so that she begin the day's chores. She hastened away from her unrolled bedding as a distant voice called out "Fresh fish!"

Tomiko hurried to the front door of her home. She paused briefly before her mirror to quickly check that she was presentable. She already had her *kimono* wrapped around her body and now she forced her bird-like feet into a pair of shoes, grumbling as she did so at the confinement, as uncomfortable as it was necessary.

"Fresh fish!"

She opened her door. "*Konichi-wa,* Yasuki." She bowed politely to him.

"*Konichi-wa*, Tomiko." The *bote-uri* offered her a polite bow of greeting in return. "Are you interested in the contents of my basket?" he asked her.

"Always." She smiled at her door-to-door salesman. Every morning Yasuki bought a large amount of fish in the Nihonbashi *Uo-ichi* wholesale fish market, put it into baskets suspended on either end of a long pole which he carried over his shoulders, and then set off to wander the neighbourhoods of Edo and sell. *I have seen him every morning for years and he always brings good stock.* "What is the best catch?"

"The prawns on this day. They are still wiggling."

"I will take some then." She handed him some coins as he selected suitable prawns for her. "Yes, they do look good. *Domo arigato.*" She closed the door behind her.

Tomiko had only just finished preparing the prawns when someone knocked politely at the door.

Curious, Tomiko slid the *shoji* screen open and peered out through the window. "You are out early, Yori-*sama*," she commented with mild surprise.

Her elderly neighbour simply offered her a shrug as she looked up towards the window. "The dawn was far too nice to miss. I have been up, tending to my household since before the nightingales fell silent." She wore a bright lilac *kimono*, and a few artful touches of make-up on her face. Her thinning grey hair was drawn back in a simple bun.

"I, too, listened to the singing of the nightingale." Tomiko enjoyed the soft sound of the night birds. "The sound reminds me of my childhood."

"Mine as well. Though my childhood days were many long winters back. I have brought you fresh-baked rice cakes." She held up a small tray.

"You are too kind to me, Yori-*sama*."

"Nonsense. You are like a daughter to me."

"A moment." Leaving the window, Tomiko hurried to the front door and quickly opened it. "Please enter." She offered a polite bow.

Yori hobbled in, taking each step as slowly and carefully as befitted someone who had seen so many winters. Her eyes, however, were still bright with life and a smile played at her lips. "I hope you will enjoy them."

"*Domo arigato*." Tomiko accepted the small tray. She had lost track of whether the porcelain tray was hers or Yori's. *We've been trading it back and forth for so long after all. Rice cakes from her. Fruits from me.*

"Shall we go out and talk in the garden?"

"Of course." Tomiko briefly wondered at her appearance—a lack of make-up and only a thin *kimono* wrapped around her frame—but her neighbour was elderly and more than half-blind. *What harm is there now? Who would she tell if she finally see the truth of me after so long?* She gestured to one of the doorways. "You know the way by now." *She has walked it so many times.* "Shall I make tea?"

"Only if it is no trouble."

"It is never any trouble for you."

Yori smiled and stepped carefully towards the patio door, with Tomiko following. "I did not plan to stay for long. No doubt you have much to do."

"I am at leisure today. Tonight I might venture out to meet with friends for a small gathering. I would be pleased to spend some of my time with you."

"You honour an old woman whose own family have already scattered into the streets." Yori paused, allowing her eyes to once again grow accustomed to the brightness of the sun. "I have always enjoyed your garden. You match the colours with scents and sounds in just a perfect balance."

"Thank you." Tomiko turned towards some of her blossoms. "Please, let me send you some of these to sweeten your home."

Yori stared at the bundle of just-cut chrysanthemums. "*Domo arigato,*" she replied with a bow.

"I will brew us some tea." Tomiko hurried back inside.

* * *

"I am Minamoto Yoshitsune of Kumagaya!"

Farther up the twilight-lit street, two men paused, then turned back towards the speaker. "And we should know that name because?" The man's accent was heavy and silibrant. Both were wearing *hakama*—loose pants with slits down the side for easy movement, tied at the waist with a jade-coloured sash—and open-fronted *haori*.

"You bandits all but destroyed my village," Yoshitsune snarled as he stalked towards the two men.

Perched on the edge of the rooftop of a *machiya*, Tomiko watched the rapidly brewing altercation with grim amusement. *It's the cute boy from the marketplace,* she abruptly realized. She hoped that he survived the encounter. *Why challenge these two?* she wondered with a frown. *They're ever so much bigger than you.*

"You slaughtered my family and friends." Yoshitsune drew his *katana* in a single motion. "I will have your blood in payment of my loss."

The two men looked at each other and both of them burst into laughter. Both were tall and slender, with sharp features and unblinking eyes.

Another duel, Tomiko thought from her perch. *How boring. There are duels fought almost daily in the city. Could you not resolve this disagreement some other way?* For this, she had stopped her journey home? *Cute boy or not, I desire the peace of my futon.*

"Is that so?" The speaker practically hissed those words.

The other man drew a curved sword from his belt. "You will regret challenging us, boy." He shared the other bandit's unusual accent, and he was taller by a hand.

Is that a scimitar? Tomiko thought in surprise. Her eyes had gone wide and she felt a sudden chill in her bones. The impending duel now had her full attention. *That is not a weapon favoured by any true Japanese warrior.* Her dark eyes narrowed. *These are not ordinary bandits.*

"I regret nothing save the length of time it has taken to find you." Yoshitsune charged. His *katana* struck against the taller man's scimitar with a clang.

Tomiko watched the fight with renewed interest. The so-called bandit moved like a snake, his motions both sinuous and swift. By contrast, the boy—Yoshitsune?—looked clumsy and slow.

The two locked blades, straining with one another.

The bandit bared his teeth. "Run away, boy, and we grant you your life."

"No!" Yoshitsune snarled back as he shifted his stance and they broke apart. "I will not run."

"Then we cannot spare your life."

The two locked blades again, straining against each other, dust from the street swirling about their legs.

The other man pulled a serpentine dagger from his jade *obi*. His eyes glittered in the moonlight.

"It ends now." The scimitar-wielding man lunged forward.

Yoshitsune blocked the scimitar and then took a step back, whirling on his heel and turning his defensive move into a fierce swing that cut through the dagger holder's stomach.

The man fell to the ground with a hissing cry.

The man with the scimitar spat a venomous sounding curse, and then swung his own blade. The flat of the blade caught Yoshitsune's head and knocked him to the ground. The accused bandit stooped over the fallen man, savouring his soon-to-be-made kill.

"That's enough!" Tomiko dropped from the roof onto the street below, controlling her glide with her outspread cloak. "Leave him alone!" She landed in the dust on her bare feet, her pale silk *kimono* falling back into place.

The man looked at her with those unblinking eyes, clearly not concerned with how she had just appeared from the rooftops. "Go away, old woman." His voice was thin and reedy, his accent harsh.

She stared back calmly at him. Moonlight glinted on scale-like patches on his bare arms and on what could be seen of his chest through his *haori*.

He examined her in return; his unblinking eyes noting her wrinkled skin, her tripled-toed bare feet, and exceptionally long nose. They paused a moment at the bamboo *bo* staff that she held her in her right hand, but then his mouth parted in a cruel smile and a forked tongue flicked between his pointed teeth. "This one is mine."

"I want him." She noted more scaly patches on his neck, but she devoted most of her attention to the scimitar he was holding in his exceptionally long fingers.

"Why fight against us?" the man asked her. "We are kin, you and I."

Tomiko shook her head. "We are *nothing* alike," she spat back.

"So be it." He swung his scimitar and she ducked. The *bo* in her fist struck against his head and he staggered backwards. "Interfering old crow!" He took a step towards her. "You should have flown away when you had the chance."

"Then you leave me no choice." She struck again, hearing the crunch of his ribs as her staff hit.

* * *

Blinking repeatedly, Yoshitsune lifted his head from the pillow and looked around the room. It was fairly dark, with only a single candle flickering on the low table before the window. Curtains shrouded the window.

The sweet scent of incense wafted through the open door.

"You have awakened." It was a woman who spoke in concerned tones.

"Yes, I have." He sat up, and then felt his head swim. He closed his eyes tightly until the feeling passed.

"Are you injured?"

"Just a little dizzy." He opened his eyes again, more cautiously this time. The world seemed sharp, more in focus than it had the first time he had opened them. "Where am I?" He reached a hand to his head and felt the lump above his ear.

"You are safe."

The speaker *was* a woman but where was she? Yoshitsune looked around, wincing when he moved his head too quickly, but she was apparently cloaking herself in the shadows. "Why do you hide yourself from me?"

"I am shy."

"There is no need to be shy," he told her. "I think you are responsible for my being here. This is not the Street of Darting Foxes."

"No, it is not." Tomiko paused as she stared at him from the doorway. "I could not leave you laying there in the dust."

The candle flickered on the table as the breeze blew in through the window.

"Then I do have you to thank for my being here?"

"Your thanks are not necessary." Tomiko was not sure what else to say as the night breeze picked up again. "As I said before, I could not leave you there."

The candle flame caught the hem of the curtain. The fabric quickly caught fire.

"No!" Tomiko cried out.

Moving quickly, Yoshitsune sprang from the futon, grabbed the curtain, and ripped it from its rod. He threw it into the fire pit and the wood stacked there caught fire. Brighter illumination filled the room.

"No, don't light the fire!" Tomiko pleaded.

"Why not?" Yoshitsune gripped the edge of a cabinet to maintain his balance. Moving so quickly had been an action of instinct, but now he felt the after-effects in his weak knees. He blinked his eyes several times, trying to stop the room from spinning.

The glow of the firelight filled the room and she knew she could hide no longer. "This is why." With some reluctance, Tomiko stepped forward with a soft rustle from her pale silk kimono.

Yoshitsune stared at her wrinkled red skin, his eyes widening in shock. The enormous nose could not be disguised, nor could the triple toes of her bird-like feet when he gaze fell upon them.

She looked at him, sadly waiting for his response.

"You are *konsha Tengu*!" he accused in a harsh voice.

"What if I am?" she demanded. She ostentatiously adjusted the manner in which her feathered cloak hung from her shoulders. "I saved your life."

"Why?" His hand groped at his side for his missing *katana*. Abruptly, he realized that he was clad only in his *fundoshi* and he hastily snatched up blankets from his bed to cover himself.

Tomiko laughed at the sight, and then quickly stilled her expression.

"You find this amusing, *Tengu*?"

The flush in his cheeks makes him look so youthful, she thought. *He is clean-limbed as well.* She had been able to examine him while he lay unconscious. *A well-built young man indeed.*

Yoshitsune was still staring at her.

"You fear me as a demon yet you cover yourself as if you fear for your manhood. Of course I laugh." Then, suddenly she offered him a low bow. "I act without thought," she told him. "My apologies. I should not laugh at you."

Yoshitsune frowned, unsure how to respond.

Chapter Three

Tomiko stood in the doorway of the small room, silently watching the young man as he knelt on the floor beside the low table. *So young, so innocent.* She could sense it in his *ki. And in his face...he is pretty when he smiles.* The room itself was dim, with only the natural sunlight passing through the *shoji* screen on the door.

The boy had sat, unmoving, for many minutes, wrapped in one of her blankets.

Then abruptly, she minced into the room with a broad smile on her wrinkled face. "Please," she tossed him the bundle that she held in her arms, "dress yourself if it will make you feel more at ease." She left him and vanished back into the small kitchen.

The young man quickly untied the bundle and shook out his *hakama* and *haori*. He pulled on his pants first, then tied the wide-sleeved shirt with a sash, but left the front open. The *obi* that he tied around his waist was a deep red.

I have waited long enough I think. Tomiko finished filling up small bowls from pots warming above a small brazier. She placed the porcelain bowls onto a tray and returned to the room where her guest waited.

Yoshitsune was staring down at the *tatami* mat upon which he kneeled.

What troubles his mind so? Tomiko wondered. He had slept part of the night in her bed. *But only after I had withdrawn to the garden for some thinking of my own,* she noted. *So young and yet so able to lose himself within mediation.*

The talons on both of her bird-like feet clicked softly on the floorboards as she walked towards him. "You must eat." She set the lacquered tray onto the table and began to set the small porcelain bowls of rice and vegetables before her guest.

He looked up at her from his study of the *tatami* mat upon which he kneeled in *seiza* fashion. "Are you *geisha* then?"

"I am your hostess," she replied calmly. "You are my guest and I would not see you go hungry."

He eyed the food.

"It is quite safe to eat. I do not seek to poison you."

He blushed. "I am a poor guest," he apologized, bowing his head in shame. "You have saved my unworthy life and I repay your kindness with baseless suspicion." He rose to his feet in a single smooth motion and offered her a deep bow. "I am Minamoto Yoshitsune of Kumagaya."

That I already knew. "I was named Uzume Tomiko by my Clan." She returned his bow with one of her own. "Now let us eat. We may talk in greater detail later."

* * *

After their small meal, Tomiko led Yoshitsune out into her courtyard garden.

The late morning sun was warm on their skin and a faint breeze made the bamboo wind chimes clink softly.

Tomiko lifted a small leaf from the white sand and placed it into a small bucket for later disposal. *Purity and harmony*, she noted contentedly. The chrysanthemums were now fully in bloom and she could smell their scent hanging in the air. She adjusted her feather-covered cloak, although she doubted she would have much need of it later in the day.

Yoshitsune studied the stone wall which surrounded the courtyard with a pleased nod. "You have a fine yard," he commented. "Privacy and safety."

"It is typical for this neighbourhood." Both were reasons she enjoyed living in that particular house. The bamboo wind chimes clinked softly, doing more to emphasize the quiet rather than breaking it. "Why did you challenge those two men in the Street of Darting Foxes?"

"It was a matter of honour."

"Was it?"

Yoshitsune nodded. "They attacked my home. They burned half of my village to the ground last winter. I am obligated to seek vengeance for the fallen."

"Did they? Did you see their faces when they struck?"

"I recognized their *mon*."

Tomiko frowned as she recalled the encounter. Yes, both men had worn emblems proclaiming their loyalties to one of the noble houses. She searched her memory. "Two jade squiggles against a field of gold?" The *mon* had been engraved on pins attached to each man's *obi*.

"Do you know that House?" Yoshitsune asked her. His eyes were eager for her answer.

"No." She shook her head with some reluctance. *Would that I could aid him more with this.* "It is not the emblem of any noble who lives within the city. At least not one with whom I am familiar."

"Pity. I hope to learn more from the streets."

"What would you learn, Yoshitsune?"

"I would know his name. His place of residence."

Tomiko shook her head at his brave foolishness. "You barely survived the first encounter with two of this mysterious nobleman's retainers. How can you hope to survive assaulting the noble himself?"

Yoshitsune looked at her, his grey eyes narrowing. "I *will* avenge my family," he said coldly.

"Or get yourself killed."

"If that is indeed the price required by just vengeance, then that coin is what must be paid."

"You would pay any price for this vengeance you crave? You are samurai, or samurai-in-training?" Her cloak rustled as she spoke, though he stood motionless. She studied him anew. *Is he truly of the samurai class?* "Would you disturb Shogun Tokugawa Ieyasu then?"

Yoshitsune looked back at her quite boldly. "If necessary."

"You would never pass within the gates of Edo Castle." She shook her head and fluffed out her feather-covered cloak. "Better to travel to Kyoto and seek an audience with Emperor Go-K?my?."

Yoshitsune hastily cast his eyes towards the white sand covering the ground. "Show respect for the Emperor," he told her.

"Go-K?my? Tsuguhito is not Emperor of the *Tengu*," she told him in a calm voice. "He is quite human."

"And you are *konsha Tengu*!" Yoshitsune countered. He gestured towards her face and then at her feet. "Do you hold yourself apart from the rest of us?"

"I am not human, as you point out, so why should I be ruled by a human emperor?" Tomiko tossed her head back and laughed lightly. "Or why should I worry about his pet Shogun? He does not command the beasts of the forests, nor the fish of the seas."

"You live in his city. In the capitol. You live as a human. Why?"

"I live as I choose to live," she replied. "Does the reason truly matter to you so much?"

He made no answer, but turned away.

She paused for several minutes. The sun had climbed past the peak of the roof and now the garden was shaded and pleasantly cool. The boy stood staring towards the back wall. *He has a strong chin and nose. A strong profile...but so stern, so sad.* "I have heard some words while I was visiting the marketplace today." She had ventured out to purchase food for their lunch while Yoshitsune had still been sleeping.

He remained silent, staring at her well-tended flowerbeds.

"You might be interested in hearing that no one has reported finding any bodies."

"They were just bandits."

"And now they are just corpses, left laying in the Street of Darting Foxes."

Yoshitsune slowly turned his head and looked directly at his hostess. "And you say that the *yoriki* did not find them?"

Tomiko slowly shook her head.

Yoshitsune muttered a soft curse.

"Indeed," Tomiko agreed with the sentiment. "The two men we killed were left in a public street. One of the night patrols should have found them within hours of the attack." *Really,* she thought, *it should have been much sooner. We were truly lucky to have not been discovered during the duel. The street patrol should have come by to investigate the noise.* Yoshitsune had certainly not been quiet in his challenge, nor in the duel. "As I said, I have been to the local market. There should have been rumours and talk of the bodies being found." *Especially of those most peculiar looking bodies.* She spread her arms in puzzlement. "There is no talk."

"They *have* been discovered?"

"It *was* a public street, Yoshitsune." *A minor street true, but people would be using it come morning.* "I passed by that very way on my home from the market. It was empty, with no sign of our struggle."

"You took no actions with them?"

"I was busy carrying you back here to rest and recover from your injury."

At that, he lifted a hand to rub at his head.

"I left the two corpses where they lay," Tomiko continued. With the numerous gates closed at night, sealing off individual neighbourhoods and limiting traffic, it had not been worth the effort to try to move the bodies. "The *yoriki* should have found them and reported it. There should be some talk and yet there is *none*." It almost made her head hurt thinking about it. "I cannot explain this."

Yoshitsune lowered his gaze to the ground. "You have shamed me by slaying those I could not."

"They were not ordinary men," she told him. "They were...different." And word of their corpses should have been making the rounds of the streets and markets. Someone was covering up their deaths.

* * *

"Never another *Tengu* around when you want one." Tomiko kicked at a snake as it slithered past her feet. It lifted its head and hissed at her. She ignored it and turned to stare into a cistern. "Benkei!" she called out.

The water collected in the cistern remained motionless.

"Is this what you were warning me about?" Tomiko demanded. "Is Yoshitsune part of some plot? Benkei, I know you can hear me!" She slammed her fist into the water with a frustrated snarl as no answer came to her. "Damn him." She turned back towards her home.

Stepping out of the alley, she took note of the handful of people moving about the street. This had been her home for many, many years and she knew everyone for blocks around by sight at least.

"*Konnichi-wa*, Tomiko-san."

"*Konnichi-wa*, Saito." She offered Michinori Saito a polite nod in addition to her greeting. "A very fine morning."

"It is that indeed." The old rice merchant smiled warmly at her. He was at the end of a long and prosperous career, having turned most of his day-to-day business over to his eldest son. Now he was content to wander the neighbourhood and talk with his neighbours.

Not that all his walking does much to reduce his stomach, Tomiko thought with an inner smile as she noted the straining of his *kimono*. *If his business prospered as much as his girth, then he would own most of Edo by now.* "Have you slept well?"

"Well enough. The harvest comes soon and it will be a busy time."

"The rice harvest always is."

Saito rested his hands on his enormous belly. He looked extremely content with life in general. "My son will have his work cut out for him this year."

"*So ka*? You are truly retired then?"

"Yes, Tomiko, at long last I have indeed withdrawn from the marketing trade. Kendashi will have to bargain with the Shogun's buying agents. The profits of our house will rise or fall on his skills alone."

Tomiko nodded her agreement, though she doubted that Saito would truly leave the bargaining entirely up to his son. *He would worry far too much.* The Shogunate bought up vast quantities of rice and stored it in the city granaries, and then used a rice measure to regulate the country's economy. "You have explained the system to me many times, Saito, though I still do not fully understand it all. It is just so complex." She offered him a shy smile.

The old man smiled indulgently at her. "It is a complex web," he agreed, "but you need not concern yourself with the details. It is enough that you have coin with which to purchase rice for your own table."

"I always have coin enough," she replied. *Even if I lack the husband everyone believes died before I moved here.*

Saito's smile grew even wider and he rested his hand softly on her shoulder. "Do not squander all of your wealth, Tomiko. It has been a long time since you last wore widow's white."

Tomiko laughed politely. "Of course, Saito."

"I can still recall the day you took residence in that house you bought. You and I were still young then." His brown eyes had glazed over with fond memories. "That must have been...what, twenty summers past?"

"Surely not that long," she replied hastily. *I have overstayed my welcome here,* she thought sadly. *Soon I must move on before my heritage becomes known to all. They will know me for what I am, as Yoshitsune does, and they will fear me.* It was a sad, though true, fact that her people were feared.

Saito had continued talking. "I have often thought that your face is most striking."

My nose *is striking you mean.* She hated the beak-like nose common to her race and wished that she could make it disappear. *Sadly, that is no easier done than changing my feet,* she thought in bitter amusement. "I must go...I, I have a guest awaiting my return."

Saito's dark eyes narrowed. "A young man from what the common rumour mongers claim." His voice mingled distaste with annoyance.

"A guest only. He will only be staying with me for a short time," Tomiko told him quickly. *And look at his eyes widen along with that smile.* Toying with his feelings had been a fine distraction, but perhaps it was growing more serious? *Only for him,* she told herself. *My own feelings remain my own.* "Good day, Saito."

He blinked twice, then nodded and offered her a polite bow. "Good day to you as well, Tomiko. I look forward to our next meeting."

"As do I."

Chapter Four

Yoshitsune was seated in the garden when Tomiko stepped through the door. "You are still here?"

"You sound surprised."

"I am." *Though also happy that you are still here.* "I had thought that you might have left while I was away. I had more than half-expected that you would have returned to the streets in search of your mysterious noble."

"I considered it," he admitted.

Tomiko stared at him.

"I did consider it, but I fell into thought and the day flew past. I knew that you would return soon and I did not wish to leave without a word." He paused and licked at his lips. "You have been very kind to me, Tomiko. You saved my life and that is a debt I would repay."

She waved her hand dismissively. "You need not worry about such a debt."

"I must."

"It was nothing."

"My life is yours."

She smiled at his insistence. "Your life is entirely your own, Yoshitsune. I have my own life that I live and I cannot live yours for you."

He smiled at her.

He has a pretty smile, she thought. *For a human*, she added hastily. *A young man, barely out of boyhood.* She was old enough to be his grandmother!

"There was a visitor while you out. Yori has brought you some rice cakes."

More rice-cakes? Tomiko finished removing her shoes and allowed her bird-like toes to stretch out in their normal spread. "Did she now?" She sighed with relief. *I hate those cramped shoes!*

"Yes. We had a nice little chat."

Tomiko carried out a small bottle of *sake* and two cups from the house and sank to her knees in a single smooth motion that belied her apparent age. "What did you two talk about?" she asked as she poured them small cups of *sake*.

"This and that. She did most of the talking, and it was almost entirely about people I've never met. Neighbours and relatives. She thought I was your grandson."

Tomiko smiled. *I see how the rumours of my visitor have begun spreading then. Yori gossips with everyone.* "Yes, she would think that."

"She was happy to see that you had company staying with you. She seems to think that you are in danger as you live alone."

"Yori worries far too much about me." It was pleasing though. *I will miss her dearly when she has passed on.* "We have grown fond of each other over the years." *Perhaps I truly have dwelled here for too long.*

Yoshitsune drank his *sake*. "Do your neighbours know?" he asked her.

"About my heritage?" She shook her head as the wind chimes clinked softly. "Of course not. None of them do."

"Not even Yori?"

"Not even Yori. I value my privacy."

"I will keep your secret."

"*Domo arigato.*" It was a chore at times to maintain the illusion that she was fully human, but it was necessary. "I value their friendship. Many fear the *Tengu.*"

"Your kinfolk torment many of those who dwell in the mountains."

"The mountains were our homes first," she protested. "It is only natural that we should seek to defend our homes from encroachment."

Yoshitsune nodded. "I must agree with that."

"Granted," Tomiko added, "that we still do torment some deserving souls, but seldom have we ever engaged in open warfare." There was an uneasy truce in most of the mountains now...with the villagers often leaving offerings of food or gifts to placate their *Tengu* neighbours.

"I need to retrieve my sword."

Tomiko refilled her cup and took a sip. "It is lost to you," she told him sadly. "I never thought to grab it when I was carrying you home the other night."

"I need it!" Yoshitsune sprang to his feet. "I must avenge my honour."

"It is lost to you."

"Foolish woman. You should have recovered it with me."

Tomiko frowned and rose to her own feet. "Are you truly samurai then? Do you seek to place *giri* before *ninjo*?"

"If *you* were samurai, you would know that *bushido* demands that we place always duty before sympathy."

"*So ka?*" *Is that truly so?* "You can do little of either for now."

"I must do something."

"You must rest further and recover your strength."

Yoshitsune snorted. "Waiting is hard."

"Yes," she shot back, "because dying is easier!" She blinked at her own outburst, then turned and fled into the house leaving Yoshitsune to stare after her.

* * *

Yoshitsune was adjusting the folds of his *haori* as he stepped through the doorway. "We must venture into the streets." He gave his *obi* a tug to tighten it.

"*We* must?" she asked him, tilting her head to the left in a particularly bird-like fashion. The rest of the day had passed quietly and now the sun was setting and the twilight was coming on. *It does pass by quickly when you fall asleep when you mean to be adding embroidery to the hem of a kimono.*

"Well, *I* must," Yoshitsune amended.

Tomiko carefully set the *kimono* onto the floor. "The streets in this neighbourhood are safe enough to travel alone. Our band of *yoriki* patrols with much vigilance. The neighbours keep a sharp watch as well on those who travel the streets by night." *Sometimes they keep too good a watch! The steps I must take to avoid being seen at times....* She shook her head, trying not to think about the number of times she had travelled along the rooftops. "Do you seek to find more of these bandits whom you claim attacked your village?"

"That claim is but harsh truth. Men came bearing that *mon* and my village burned before they left."

"You have my sympathies."

He shook his head. "I search, but without clues or knowledge of their location."

"Then you will simply wander the streets of Edo?"

"I have more plan than that."

So, he is not all muscle and no brain. Tomiko had known far too many samurai who thought with their swords alone. *It is good to see him think beyond the blade.* "Then how will you find them?"

"I must meet with an old friend. It is the night of the full moon."

"That it is." The moon had not yet risen, but it promised to be a bright night.

"I promised to meet him at *The Fluttering Lotus Blossom* tonight."

"It should be safe enough for you to travel there." She nodded to him. "Take care of yourself."

The young man chewed at his lip for a moment. "I had rather hoped that you would accompany me, Tomiko." Yoshitsune paused awkwardly. "Your presence would be most welcomed. By me at least."

She stared at him for a long moment. Then she nodded. "Very well."

* * *

The two passed through the *Toranomon* gate and into the city proper.

"I am not familiar with *The Fluttering Lotus Blossom*," Tomiko admitted as they passed by a group of a dozen *yoriki*.

The men of the patrol nodded politely to her and her companion. They each wore a sash *obi* with the emblem of the *yoriki* on it to proclaim their jobs, along with their right to bear both *bo* and swords while they patrolled the streets and maintained order and peace.

"It lies just beyond the Tiger Gate." Yoshitsune walked ahead confidently. "I have been there one time before."

Tomiko followed him. "Lead on then."

The streets were still busy. Nightlife in this part of Edo was often boisterous and the streets remained crowded well past sundown.

"It should be just down here." Yoshitsune led her through an open gateway flanked by flickering torches. The flames made shadows dance on the buildings.

Tomiko took a moment to glance at the men guarding the gate. One of them had striking eyes that seemed to gleam in the torchlight. When night fell, gates along all of Edo's main streets would be closed and divide the city into distinct blocks. *It does help cut down on disturbances,* she admitted to herself. Troublemakers were confined to single neighbourhoods that way.

"The city stays awake so much later than my village," Yoshitsune commented as they walked past a noisy teahouse.

"We are not tied to the cycles of the earth as farmers are." Tomiko turned her head to give the gate wardens another look, but the man with those striking green eyes was gone. "We make our own rhythms."

Abruptly, Yoshitsune stopped, whirled around, and offered her a low bow. "Tomiko, I find that I must apologize to you."

"Oh?" she said, her eyes going wide.

"This morning I was rude to you. I was upset at the loss of my sword. My family has long trained as warriors, though we are but among the poorest ranks of samurai. Our swords are...extensions of our souls. Without my blade, I am truly master less."

"I understand. If there had been more time, perhaps I might have been able to recover your blade."

He grimaced and turned away.

* * *

The *shoji* screen moved silently and opened into a tavern, lit by many lanterns. Scatterings of low tables were placed throughout the room. A waitress with a wide smile and a spotless *kimono* bowed towards them as they entered.

"It is a quiet place." Tomiko noted only two patrons were present.

"Shinzu." Yoshitsune paced towards the old man kneeling on a *tatami* mat at one of the low tables.

Paper and ink waited at the old man's elbow. They both looked untouched. "Join me," he offered as Yoshitsune and Tomiko approached his table. The dull grey of his kimono looked drab. "My muse speaks not to me. There will be no treasures to mark this night's passing."

Yoshitsune kneeled beside the table. "Your *haikai* are as valued like pearls, *Sensei*. Their lack will be felt keenly."

"There will be other nights." Shinzu gestured the serving girl forward and she brought fresh *sake*. "You still seek word of the Cult?" he asked with hooded eyes after she had bowed to them and then left to attend to the only other patron in the tavern.

"Yes, I do."

"You have a new companion it seems."

"Uzume Tomiko." She offered him a polite nod.

His dark eyes flicked across her quickly, but she suspected that he could sketch her likeness accurately on his parchment. His eyes had widened only slightly at the sight of her over-large nose. Shinzu turned towards Yoshitsune. "Are you certain that you wish her to become involved with this affair?"

"Tomiko is already involved. She was present when I encountered two of the Cultist bandits."

Shinzu eyed her again with a more openly measuring stare.

Unabashed, Tomiko stared right back at him. "I can take care of myself."

"Yes, no doubt *you* can." Shinzu sipped at his warm *sake*. "The *Naga* Cult," he said in a soft tone, "however, is a very dangerous one indeed. Far more insidious than anything you have encountered, Yoshitsune."

"I can handle the snakes."

"Can you?" Shinzu slowly shook his clean-shaven head. "I have heard terrible rumours from amongst those I cultivate."

"*Sensei*, you move among many circles. I trust you to know what is going on throughout Edo." Yoshitsune paused a moment longer. "Even events transpiring in the farthest corners of Japan make themselves known to you."

"Oh, I know much of what is happening in Edo. The nobles are scheming against the Shogun and against each other. Agents of the Emperor seek to disrupt alliances before they can grow solid. *Daimyos* plot to become the next shogun. Edo seethes with political games. It always has."

"But what of the Cult?"

"Indeed...into the mix that is Edo, what of this new Cult?" Shinzu downed the contents of his cup. "They are growing more open...waving their *mon*."

"What emblem?" Yoshitsune asked.

"Two jade squiggles against a golden field."

Tomiko frowned. "It is a not a noble house I recognize. I do not profess to name every family of noble blood, but that *mon* is unknown."

"It belongs to no noble family. It is purely a symbol of their damnable Cult."

Yoshitsune sighed. "The cult of snakes grows more bold."

"Indeed. A man spoke rumours to me one night...." Shinzu paused and stared into his empty cup. "These *Naga* are plotting to overthrow the Tokugawa Shogunate."

Yoshitsune gasped.

Tomiko shrugged and refilled her own *sake* cup. "Tokugawa Ieyasu has samurai enough to protect himself, even from these *Naga*."

Shinzu turned his head to look at her. "They won't be enough, Tomiko. Lady Saris Taira has been scheming to overthrow him for almost fifty years."

"Since Ieyasu first established the Shogunate?" Yoshitsune gulped at his rice wine and then coughed.

Tomiko glanced towards her companion.

"At least that long," Shinzu replied calmly. "No doubt she had plotted against the warlords before Tokugawa took power. From the whispered rumours I have overhead, the *Naga* have schemed against the past hundred and nine emperors as well. They will plot against the hundred and tenth and his Shogun just as easily."

Tomiko refilled his cup and watched the other patron leave.

"Those who whispered to me of such dark things will tell no more tales...all have succumbed to poison." He paused, and then smiled before taking a sip from his refilled cup of *sake*. "I do not believe Saris will leave anything to chance given the scope of her scheming." He peered over the rim of his cup at Tomiko.

"What will she do?" Yoshitsune demanded.

"I do not yet possess that piece of information," the old man admitted. "It will come to my ears in time...though I do not know if the time will be soon enough for us to take action against her."

Tomiko shook her head. She reached over and placed her hand on her companion's shoulder. "We waste our time, Yoshitsune. He can us nothing save rumours."

He shook off her hand. "Shinzu first led me to the Cult," he told her. "He was a close ally of my father, my teacher when I was young. I trust him above all others."

"Then take this warning of his to the Shogun. Why risk your life?"

"A man must do as his honour demands."

Tomiko sighed. *Always their honour!*

"Would the Shogun believe a lower-class samurai?" Shinzu paused. "Or a poet?"

Reconsidering her words, Tomiko shook her head. A flicker of movement caught her eye. "Get down!" Something flew past Tomiko's face even as she pushed Yoshitsune aside. Leaving Yoshitsune on the floor, she lunged at the doorway.

Running footsteps greeted her ears. "*Baka!*" she snarled.

The street was already deserted.

"He's dead!" Yoshitsune exclaimed.

Tomiko turned around. An arrow was sticking through the old man's chest.

"He just toppled over in mid-word." Yoshitsune seemed surprised.

"Poison." Tomiko looked around, but the street was as deserted as the teahouse. "Where is the hostess?" She had vanished as well.

"How do you know it was poison?"

"He died too quietly for a single arrow. There was no cry of pain." She pulled the arrow from the corpse and sniffed at its tip. "I do not recognize the scent," she admitted with a frown. "I do not like this." She pulled Yoshitsune to his feet. "We must leave here," she ordered. "This place is no longer safe for us."

"How much did you trust Shinzu?" Tomiko set a hard pace, not quite running as that would attract undue attention, but still striding briskly along the street at a ground-eating speed. *They have not yet closed the district gates...though I fear we will not reach home in time.* Her feet were paining her yet again. *I hate these damned shoes!*

"He was from my village." Yoshitsune was panting from the exertion. "He lived there for many years. He left after the plague struck...oh, ten winters back or so."

"He survived the plague?"

"A quarter of the village did not. I was very ill and he ministered to me, as well as to many others. He was a valued retainer of my father." Yoshitsune stared at a flickering torch as they passed by. "He came to Edo to teach others the art of *haikai*."

"I am familiar with some of that linked verse poetry. Some of the masters are very evocative."

"And now he's dead."

Tomiko heard the bitterness in his voice. "We face a dangerous foe." She nodded to a group of *yoriki* as they passed. "These *Naga* probably heard that he was inquiring into their business...we must be cautious, Yoshitsune. They might come after us next."

"That is why I need a sword."

"A proper blade will not be easily obtained."

"I cannot defend myself with bare hands."

"True." Tomiko nodded at his words.

Chapter Five

"Eat this." Tomiko tossed Yoshitsune a ripe plum. "We will find our breakfast elsewhere." She bowed politely to the *bote-uri* who returned the bow, and then shouldered his baskets and continued down the street crying out his wears. There were many of the salesmen and peddlers on the street.

Yoshitsune obediently ate the plum. "What are we doing, Tomiko?" he asked her between bites.

"We need to come up with a suitable plan." She was walking along the streets with a purposeful gait, her red *kimono* cinched at the waist with a golden *obi*. *So far, my feet feel fine.* That feeling wouldn't last of course. *These shoes will hurt my feet before the day is half-done, but what choice do I have? Anyone who sees my feet would know me for what I am.* She gripped her *bo* in a tight grip and relied upon it for balance. *Today I more than feel my age*, she thought grimly. *I must be getting too old to be throwing men around taverns.*

"A plan?"

"We cannot wander the streets of Edo aimlessly searching for signs of this snake cult." Tomiko gestured to him to follow, then continued down the street. "Come along." She turned south and walked towards the pier districts. "The sea air in the *kashi* always helps me to think more clearly."

Yoshitsune followed as the great Nihonbashi Bridge came into sight. It arced above the Nihonbashi canal and he paused for a moment to stare at the sight. The bridge was certainly a sight worth looking at, with ornate images carved into its framework. The waterway linked the Sumida River with the moat surrounding Edo Castle.

The great square beside the Nihonbashi was one of the most important public squares in the whole city. Tomiko always loved wandering there, as it was located next to one of the biggest *kashi* in Edo. Most of the ocean-going ships that brought goods to Edo unloaded their cargoes onto smaller barges and *takase-bune* in one of the main ports, like Shiba or Tsukiji, and their products were then carried up the rivers and canals to specific pier districts. Each of Edo's districts specialized in receiving and selling a specific kind of product, since this proved more efficient for the unloading, and also allowed merchants to control the market more easily.

"We stand at the very centre of Japan."

Startled, Yoshitsune looked at her.

"Surely you are aware of the importance of this bridge." At his blank look, Tomiko shook her head with an indulgent smile on her wrinkled face. While the two stood there, the still-moving crowd broke around them like the river did around boulders. "When Tokugawa Ieyasu set up his agency to supervise the road system throughout Japan, he needed a starting point for the network of mileage markers."

"I have seen those markers in my travels," Yoshitsune told her in a proud voice. "They stand every few kilometres, giving the distance to the next town, as well as the distance to the major cities."

"Yes, measuring out that distance from *this* bridge." Ieyasu had completed work on the Nihonbashi in sixteen oh three, some fifty-four years back, and decided that this bridge would be used as the official centre point for all mileage markers in the country. "We stand at the official starting point for the *Tokaido*, the *Oshu Kaido,* the *Nikko Kaido* and the *Mito Kaido*." She gestured in turn to each of the four roadways that led away from the square.

"Are we going to the *Kanda no kashi*?" Yoshitsune asked.

"Do you wish fresh fruit?" she asked him. The Kanda pier district catered to the wholesalers of fruits. "Would the *Naga* deal with cloth and clothing? Should we venture to the *kawashi* in Suruga-machi?"

"I do not know." He shook his head. "Shinzu never told us where they schemed. If indeed he even knew that." The capitol city was a huge place with tens of thousands, if not a full million, inhabitants. "However, will we find the Cult? We cannot simply wander through the city looking for men wearing the *mon* of Lady Saris." He paused for a moment, scanning the crowd with his eyes. "Which is what I have been doing with such little success," he admitted with a frown.

"No, we cannot do that alone, but we shall start searching here." Tomiko gestured towards the pier. "The Nihonbashi pier handles seafood."

"You think they like seafood?"

"No, but I do." She laughed softly at his startled expression. The public square was home to a vast fish market, selling every type of seafood one could possibly imagine. "And furthermore, the Nihonbashi *Uo-ichi* is located at an important crossroad for roads and canals, and it is definitely one of the busiest squares in the city."

"You think to learn something here?"

"We will learn much by listening to the gossip. The *Tokaido* begins in this square, and the main road north from Edo—the *Oshu-kaido*—begins on the opposite side of the canal." Tomiko wandered into the thick crowds. "Truly, everyone in Edo comes through here at some point." She moved towards the piers beside the Bridge.

Stone steps led down to the water's edge, and strong men made their way up and down these terraces carrying large baskets of seafood from the boats to the wholesale shops in the square.

Tomiko inhaled deeply. The air was heavy with the scent of the water and of fish. "I could stand here and watch the comings and goings of the people all day."

"I would find that boring."

"You are still young, Yoshitsune. Someday you will learn to savour life."

"Yes, when I am old and grey." His cheeks flushed. "Tomiko, what do you hope to learn by standing here?"

"We will learn patience to start with." She chuckled as his face flushed even more. "I am waiting for one of the wholesalers."

"You are?"

"Yes." She studied the faces on a group of men as they approached. "The majority of people in this square are wholesalers who have come to buy large loads of fish or other produce. They will carry it back to their own stores in each part of the city and resell it to the local residents."

"And the others?"

"Some are purchasing food for their *chaya*." The teahouses and restaurants always required a steady supply of fresh foods. "No doubt you will see servants for the estates of the *daimyos* here as well. Possibly even the *Shogun*."

"I doubt the *Shogun* would appear in a fish market."

"No, he will not, but his servants will. Of all the markets, the Nihonbashi *Uo-ichi* is the best in Edo. Trust me."

* * *

Hours later, Yoshitsune proclaimed that he was sick of the smell of fish.

Tomiko turned away from examining a lobster. "We should withdraw and eat."

"But not fish!"

Tomiko laughed at him. "No? Even after seeing how fresh it is?"

Yoshitsune shook his head again.

"Then no fish. Walk this way with me and we will find something else upon which to dine." She waved him towards a small *chaya* which was just down a short alley. "The food here is good. I have dined here quite often." Like most of Edo's residents, Tomiko found it far easier to eat out than to prepare meals at home.

A smiling waitress approached them as the entered the small teahouse. Her pink *kimono* was embroidered with red cherry blossoms. "Good to you both."

"Good day." Tomiko followed her towards a table. She knelt down, *seiza*-style. "Bring sweets for us both. We have quite an appetite today."

Tomiko gestured towards Yoshitsune as he also knelt. "Some *kushi-dango* I think."

Yoshitsune nodded, as his mouth suddenly watered.

The serving girl hurried away towards the back of the *chaya*. Within moments, she returned and set a tray onto the table, bowed, and then left them.

Tomiko inhaled the scent of the *kushi*-dango. The little skewers of steamed rice dumplings came with a sweet honey-coloured sauce. They smelled divine. "The chef here is a master of his craft," she explained. "His *satsuma-ino* and *kuri-kinton* are too die for." She blushed. "I forget myself perhaps."

Yoshitsune was smiling. "No, you should order for us. You know the dishes here. You know which ones are best."

"This is a part of Edo to which I have often traveled." She smiled across the table at him. "The food here is well worth the walk."

They ate.

* * *

Later that afternoon, returning to Tomiko's home, the two strolled past the Temple of Asakusa.

"It seems as though that Temple was built just yesterday," Tomiko commented wistfully. She stopped to stare at the building. It exuded a sense of peace.

"It was constructed in six forty-four."

"Was it really?" Tomiko was surprised that her young companion knew that fact. "How time flies...like the fluttering of birds' wings."

Yoshitsune shook his head.

Tomiko caught the gesture from the corner of her eye. *He grows discouraged. A day spent in the markets and we have learned nothing new about these Naga. How like youth to be impatient and seeking the immediate answers. I fear the hunt will take much longer.* Tomiko doubted that the Naga cult would be easily uncovered. *Not if they have already been plotting for fifty plus years, as Shinzu claims.* "Let us pause a moment to pray."

"All right." Yoshitsune nodded his head. "It cannot hurt."

They stepped into the shrine, ancient floorboards creaking softly under their feet. Candles burned before several small altars. The scent of jasmine was strong in the air, wafting from many burners. Monks chanted in the distance, though Tomiko could see no one else in the immediate area.

Yoshitsune knelt before one altar.

Tomiko wandered closer to the outer edge of the shrine before stopping in front of another altar. The window beyond formed a frame for a centuries-old pine tree. The *kehai*—the aura of the shrine—felt peaceful and serene to her. "Help us," she prayed aloud to any listening gods or spirits. "I do not know how to proceed."

"You did express a wish for more interest in your life," a deep voice croaked.

Her brown eyes snapped open. "Benkei!"

The crow-headed *Tengu* peered at her through the branches of the pine tree outside. The branches were swaying under his weight—he was very nearly human-sized after all. "Tomiko-san, have you begun a menagerie?" He gestured with one clawed hand towards Yoshitsune who was still lost in his own prayers. "Do you always pick up strays?" His eyes suddenly narrowed. "Are you now sharing your *futon* with a *human*?"

"That is none of your business," she snapped at him.

He clicked his toothy beak in silent laughter.

Tomiko sighed. She glanced around, but the shrine was still deserted, aside from Yoshitsune, who was still lost in thought. "Make yourself useful to me for once. What do you know about a Lady Saris Taira?"

Benkei's laughter stopped instantly and he stared at her with wide, dark eyes. "Oh, you're becoming entangled in *her* schemes are you?" He shook his head. "You do like to live dangerously."

"Are you going to tell me anything useful, or merely torment me?"

He looked at her and spread his wing-arms. "We are *Tengu,*" he chuckled. "Tormenting is one of our best talents."

"We have other talents."

"True enough." He paused, his eyes narrowing once again. "The Clan Elders are losing patience with you."

"I lost patience with *them* centuries ago."

"Then know this. The balance is shifting. Other forces are gathering throughout Japan. The *Naga* are only one small threat...though they do possess power enough to threaten even the Clans. Tomiko," his voice turned eager, "you must leave Edo. Return to the Clans. They—we—need you."

"That is a refreshing change."

"The Elders are trying, but Saris does not wish to negotiate with us." There was no mistaking the concern in his voice. "She will not respect the neutrality of any other people when she strikes at the Shogunate. Like the snake she is, she will slaughter *anyone* in her path...including *Tengu* bystanders. *Wakarimasu-ka?*"

"Oh, I understand perfectly." She shook her head sadly. "I fear that Yoshitsune needs me more. He does not have the Clans, or the magic of the *Tengu,* to protect him."

"*We* cannot protect *you*!"

"Then Yoshitsune and I will protect each other." She stood up.

"Gah!" Benkei flung himself deeper into the tree.

"What was that cry?" Yoshitsune demanded as the pine branches swayed and creaked in Benkei's abrupt departure. He hurried to Tomiko's side.

"Just a nasty old crow." Tomiko smiled at her young companion. "Come along, Yoshitsune, I think we should move on."

Chapter Six

A second morning saw Yoshitsune and Tomiko once again venturing into the streets of Edo. "Where now?" he asked.

"Perhaps we should try the Blacksmith's District."

Yoshitsune nodded his head in agreement as they mingled with the morning crowds. "That is more my neighbourhood of the city than the harbour."

Tomiko led them down the main road, past the shops. Most of the workshops were located in neighbourhoods behind the main shop fronts. To get to those neighbourhoods, they had to leave the main road and pass down the narrow side streets, through large and solid-looking gates that were locked at night to keep out troublemakers. "If Saris plots rebellion, she will need weapons."

"Unless she has her own blacksmiths."

"True." Tomiko nodded her own agreement with that statement. "The bandit you fought did not carry a *katana*, but rather a blade known as a *scimitar*." She frowned in thought, and the wrinkles on her forehead deepened. "Scimitars are favoured by the men of the waterless ocean."

"I am not familiar with that land."

"It is known to some as Arabey. It is many months' journey away from here, far to the west of the Han."

Yoshitsune shrugged at her words. "The blacksmiths here in Edo would likely not be keen to forge these *scimitars* then." He stumbled over the unfamiliar word. "They would craft *katanas* and blades more favoured by samurai and the shogun."

"Yes." She studied the street with knowing eyes. Some of the apprentices watched her in return, eying her large nose she was certain. She knew that *this* was a man's district. "You must take the lead here. This is not a neighbourhood I visit often." *In fact, I don't think I have ever walked these particular streets before.*

Yoshitsune eagerly questioned several of the apprentices about visits by men with strange accents, all to no avail. He looked discouraged after an hour, but continued to ask anyone who pause as he approached.

Leaving Yoshitsune to his task, Tomiko watched men smelting steel in a large, open-air furnace. She had a vague understanding that the production of a high-quality steel product, such as a sword, was a very painstaking job.

"First, the steel ingot must be produced by smelting iron," Yoshitsune told her after he watched her stare at the forge for a while. "The iron is collected in large ingots, and stored in a warehouse until it is needed. When the time comes to produce a sword, the smith heats the ingot and breaks off a piece of the proper size. This is then heated repeatedly and beaten into shape using heavy hammers. The job often requires two people—one to heat and hold the steel, and the other to swing the heavy hammer to beat it into shape."

Tomiko could see two men working hard on a blade, just as Yoshitsune described to her. "How do you know this?"

"I have studied many arts," Yoshitsune replied modestly.

"I see."

"Shinzu was a well-travelled teacher. My father insisted that all of his sons should be educated men."

"You come from an interesting village then."

Yoshitsune ignored the comment. "I am told that it takes a great deal of practice and skill to shape the sword just right."

"No doubt." Tomiko paused. "Any task would require practice and skill to master. And there is little point in learning an art if one does not seek mastery."

They watched another smith working at his forge.

"Why is he covering that blade with clay?" Tomiko asked.

"I believe it has something to do with controlling the rate of cooling."

"It is very complicated. I can see why an apprentice must serve a master for ten years or more before setting up a forge of his own." She chuckled. "And another group of craftsmen will later fashion the decorated wooden handle and the scabbard for the blade?"

"Yes. It will make for a beautiful and deadly weapon." Yoshitsune was eying it with open hunger.

"You cannot afford a blade here," Tomiko told him sadly. She had seen the contents of his purse, and there were few coins within it.

Yoshitsune nodded reluctantly. "I need more than a knife!" he complained. "I cannot defend us from Naga assassins with just this." He slapped the hilt of the *tanto* he had stuffed into his *obi* earlier that morning.

"That dagger is an heirloom of my Clan," Tomiko told him primly. "It is far older than Shinzu's grandfather!"

Yoshitsune looked suitably abashed. "I am sorry," he apologized. "I spoke without thinking."

"Apology accepted."

"I will wield this blade with all respect that I can manage." He gave the dagger's hilt a closer look than he had done previously when she had given it to him before leaving her house. "I cannot read the writing."

"That is because you do not speak the language of the *Tengu*." She smiled. "The katakana names the blade *Ember*."

"Then I will hope that this *ember* will help to kindle a fire to thwart Saris."

"We can hope so."

Yoshitsune paused to ask a passing woman if she knew anything of Saris's *mon*. After she had shaken her head sadly, she hurried on. "Blacksmiths are held in high esteem," Yoshitsune commented as they continued on their way. "Different crafts have higher or lower status, depending on the importance of the work. Potters and weavers hold a rank somewhere in the middle of the hierarchy."

"Do they?"

"Yes. People who make sandals, *tatami* floor mats, or other goods made from straw tend to have lower status. Carpenters and smiths have the highest status, since their skills are the most valuable to the Shogun. Blacksmiths make all sorts of useful items from steel, but the most important, of course, are the swords that they produce for the samurai."

"Everything revolves around status." Tomiko smiled. "What status would a *Tengu* have?"

"You mock me!" Yoshitsune protested.

"No, I don't."

"The inner workings of the craftsmen and their hierarchies are a mystery to me," Tomiko said. "You are more well-versed in this than I."

The young man stood straighter. "My education was quite extensive."

"I know that most apprentices are taught their trades by their fathers," Tomiko said, offering an opening.

"Others have lessons from wandering monks and other teachers, as my father insisted upon." Yoshitsune smiled at her. "Most craftsmen follow in the footsteps of their fathers, but some do change their skills. In order to take up a different craft, the youngster has to be accepted as an apprentice by one of the masters in another craft. Parents are often known to pull strings and make the arrangements."

"Even samurai?"

"Even samurai," Yoshitsune admitted. "Some low-ranking samurai will give up their status as samurai in order to become craftsmen. A step down in social rank, true, but the craft can lead to an improvement in wages. It is fair in that every apprentice starts out as a raw student, regardless of their family background, past experience, or *connections*."

Tomiko gave him a careful look. *Did you face such a question?* she wondered. *Did you consider taking up a craft?* "Would you have sought wealth over status?" she asked him. Craftsmen belonged to a lower class than farmers or samurai, and only a shade above merchants, but still....

"I never gave the matter much thought."

He's lying. Tomiko could tell.

"There is a certain level of fame associated in being especially skilled." The sound of hammers ringing in their forges was loud. "All of the best young students compete to try and become the apprentice of a master craftsmen. Master craftsmen only pass on their best techniques to the top apprentices, so when the apprentices get older they often boast about being the former student of some famous craftsman." He paused for a long moment of quiet thought. "Originally, only samurai and nobles from the Imperial court had two names, but now many of the leading craftsmen and merchant families also have been granted *honorary* second names as a reward for some service to the Shogun or some other high-ranking official and have the right to wear a sword." His hand fumbled at his *obi*.

"You truly do know far more than I about such things." Tomiko smiled. "Come."

She led him down a narrow alley and then they stepped through the gates of the Blacksmiths' District and back onto another of the main roadways.

"You were toying with me," Yoshitsune complained as they made their way through the crowd.

"Whatever do you mean, Yoshitsune?"

"You are *Tengu*."

"Yes, I am."

"The old legends in my village told us that it was the *Tengu* who first taught our honoured ancestors how to forge iron and work metal."

Tomiko looked at him and smiled.

Yoshitsune glared at her. "I have heard those stories from my grandmother, Tomiko. She would not lie to me about such matters."

"No, I do not question her honour. Not every *Tengu* is a blacksmith," she told him honestly. "I know nothing about the forging of weapons. I can sew and weave and I know some of the poetic arts."

"You know only womanly arts then?"

She remained silent.

"Do not deny that you know the skills of a warrior! You slew one of the *Naga*. You admitted it to me! I slew one, but the other beat me into unconsciousness and you saved my life...and not through womanly arts I dare think."

"I do not deny it. I have some knowledge of battle."

"Your *sensei* taught you well."

Tomiko was silent for a moment. "Perhaps you will meet him someday."

"That would be a rare honour."

They walked on.

"It grows late."

"Yes." The streets were still crowded, but Tomiko nodded. "We should return to my house for the night."

"But the search?"

"We cannot search if we are killed by assassins." She shook her head and stopped to eye the crowds passing them by. "The *Naga* have the advantage for now...they know that we are hunting them."

"We know of Lady Saris."

"Yes, but we do not know who her agents *are*. That man by the gate? That woman arguing with the *bote-uri*? One of those urchins?"

Yoshitsune eyed them each in turn. "This matter grows complicated," he admitted.

"Yes."

"I wish that Shinzu had not been murdered."

"That is a good wish. Better to wish that Saris Taira had no plans to conquer Japan." *Damn that scheming serpent! I wanted a peaceful life in this city. Now I have a war brewing and I can do nothing to stop it.* Tomiko frowned.

"Do you have any contacts you can ask?"

"We have searched for them. No one knows anything." *Or at least no one is talking.*

"We must do something!"
Tomiko spread her hands calmly. "I am open to suggestions."
Yoshitsune frowned.

Chapter Seven

"Days of searching and we are no wiser as to the lair of the *Naga,*" Yoshitsune complained.

"It will take time." Tomiko had taken Yoshitsune to visit the Potters' District since leaving the Blacksmiths. Neither the Potters, nor later the Weavers, knew anything of the *Naga* or their cult. "I had hoped that some of the craftsmen who live in the Kyobashi area might have heard rumours that would aid us."

"A foolish hope."

"No. Skilled craftsmen hear many things. People seek them out for their craft and gossip is traded like other goods. Surely the cult requires supplies, even of a mundane nature. They cannot manufacture *everything* themselves."

A fat man eyed them as they turned a corner.

"This can be a dangerous district," Yoshitsune warned her.

"I have been through here before," Tomiko replied. "Edo has been my home for many years." *But for how much longer?* She had lingered too long and she knew it. *Soon I must move on. Maybe I should venture to Kyoto where I might chance upon the Emperor.* She smiled at the thought. *Perhaps I should return to the mountains....*

"That fat man had a snake."

"Many people carry snakes and other animals." Tomiko hastily turned her head and gave the fat man another look. "I see no snake. Just his staff."

Yoshitsune frowned and looked again. "A moment ago it was twisting like a snake. I swear it."

"Hmmm."

The man slipped around the corner of an apartment building and vanished from their sight.

Yoshitsune rested his hand on the *tanto* in his *obi.* "We should follow him."

"One man out of a million? You will need to learn to identify these *Naga* better than that."

"He might wear the *mon* of Saris."

"I could not see any *mon* from here." She gestured towards one of the many *naga-ya* they were passing. "I had friends who lived in that long-house. Or was it that one?" She frowned at the second apartment building, trying to recall details. "It was a long time ago and I only visited them once or twice." A single room had been home to a family of five. *Of course, their neighbours crammed seven and eight people to one room and thought nothing of it.* "We must be cautious. The *Naga* lurk everywhere it seems and they know we hunt them."

"Perhaps we should split up and try our luck apart."

"Are you certain you wish to try that?"

"I am not afraid."

Tomiko eyed him. "The city is a dangerous place."

"I am not a child, Tomiko. I can defend myself." He rested his hand on the *tanto* in his *obi*. "I have *Ember*."

The elderly *Tengu* frowned. *Youth!* "What if you encounter the Cult?" she demanded. "A knife will not help you against bows."

"Then I will pray that they shoot poorly." He stared back at her. "You seem to worry about me quite a lot."

"I saved your life once...that links us."

Yoshitsune shrugged. "I have no plans to die."

"Good."

"The men I faced earlier carried no bows."

"The bow is not a common weapon to be seen in the streets of the capitol. Carrying it would draw eyes." Tomiko considered her outburst. "I spoke poorly."

Yoshitsune waved her apology away. "Come." He hurried towards the alley.

They moved through the press of the crowd and broke free into a narrow alley. There were squiggles of poorly written graffiti on the walls.

Tomiko paused to read some of the *katakana*.

Yoshitsune sniffed. "That's not appropriate for a lady to read."

"Nor a boy." She shook her head. "At least it's literate." Normally the markings were barely coherent. "It's almost poetic...if anatomically impossible for the shogun to do."

Something rustled further up the alley.

"We need luck if we are to find the *Naga*."

Tomiko agreed with that. "One would think that the Cult would be making a disturbance." The city had patterns in its life and the presence of strangers should be disrupting that pattern. "There is no sign that the Cult is trying to spread itself through the city. They do not seem to be recruiting from amongst the poor or the wealthy."

"Perhaps Saris is not as powerful as we fear?"

"Perhaps..." Tomiko stared back towards the street they had just left. "Your friend, Shinzu, seemed convinced that Saris was a threat. Someone else viewed him as such and killed him to silence his tongue."

"True. Have any other *Tengu* talked to you?"

"What?" Tomiko turned her head towards him.

Yoshitsune looked back at her. "I thought that if you were here, perhaps other *Tengu* were as well. Maybe they would have heard something."

"No," she shook her head. "Edo is usually avoided by my kind. They do not enjoy living amongst humans. The crowds here are too thick for those used to the emptiness of the mountains. I am somewhat unique."

Three men stepped into the alley ahead of them.

Yoshitsune and Tomiko stopped talking and stared back at them.

"She's got that big nose," said the thinnest one.

"Yep." Two of them were carrying staves. The third was apparently unarmed.

"*Konichi-wa*," Yoshitsune offered.

All three men smiled with wide grins. Two of them were missing teeth.

"I do not think this is a random encounter." Tomiko eyed them warily.

"We just want the boy," one of the men said. He had a fairly spectacular bruise on his right cheek. "If you keep your big nose out of our business, we'll leave you alone. Just gonna have to, oh, *clip* your wings."

Tomiko gripped her frail-looking *bo* and shook her head. "I'm just an old woman," she pleaded. "I have nothing to steal."

Yoshitsune drew his *tanto*. He licked his lips, but when he spoke, his voice was firm. "Do you find sport in taunting old women?" he demanded.

"Take them quickly." The youngest man turned back to the street. "Fast! Before anyone comes."

Tomiko lashed out with her staff and knocked the shortest man to the ground.

Yoshitsune ducked the staff swung at him and then stabbed the *tanto* into the wielder's chest. The bandit collapsed with a short gurgling cry.

"Damn it!" The lookout was fumbling with a straight-bladed *tanto* of his own.

Tomiko slowly walked towards him. "We have questions for you."

With a snarl, the man lunged and the dagger's blade narrowly missed her nose.

She thumped him with her staff.

He eyed her warily, now favouring his left leg.

Tomiko held her *bo* ready and the man struck.

She knocked him flat. His *tanto* flew from his hand and splashed loudly into a puddle.

Yoshitsune held the point of his own *tanto* to the man's throat. "My friend said that we had questions. I hope you have answers."

The street-tough eyed the blade with bright eyes.

"They are simple questions," Tomiko told him in a sweet tone of voice. "We shall start by asking who hired you to waylay us?"

Another rustle and they both spun around.

A tall figure wrapped entirely in a robe was staring towards them. His face was completely shadowed by his cowl, and his sleeves hid his hands. He gestured with his right hand and a greenish liquid splashed into the face of the man they had disarmed.

"Gah!" the would-be bandit cried out, then began choking. Within seconds, he fell to the ground, as limp as a filleted fish.

"Poison." Tomiko eyed the cloaked figure with considerably more caution. *A potent one too.*

"Are these your assassins?" Yoshitsune demanded. He held his bared *tanto* ready to strike.

Without a word, the robed figure turned and stepped around the corner of the alley.

"Yoshitsune, wait!" Tomiko hurried after her companion as he raced to the corner.

The street beyond was empty.

"Where did he go?"

"I don't know." He was gone though. "There are too many doors for him to have gone through." She turned around and hurried back to their unconscious attackers.

"They're all dead." Yoshitsune checked over the body of the first man Tomiko had beaten. The man he had stabbed had blood spreading across his brown *haori*.

"These are not *Naga*," Tomiko pointed out as she straightened from her own quick examination of the bodies.

Pale-faced, Yoshitsune stared down at the man he had killed. "There are no scales."

"No scales, and no hissing accent when they talked. No fancy curved scimitars either, just regular staves." She curled her lip. "These are common street thugs."

"That last one wasn't."

"No." He—was it a he?—was far more of a mystery. "That poison he used was very effective." She had never seen one so effective.

"This is a good sign."

"Is it?"

"Yes." Yoshitsune nodded.

"Then enlighten me as to the source of your joy?"

"Well, we must be getting close to uncovering the Cult if the Lady Saris is concerned enough to send assassins after us."

"*These* were hardly assassins." Simple street toughs looking for a fight? *Or a ploy by Saris to avert attention from herself.* "We should leave here before the *yoriki*." It would be difficult to explain this to the Edo authorities.

Yoshitsune followed her onto the deserted street. "Is Saris getting more ambitious?"

"Perhaps."

"They *were* looking for us."

"I know."

"It was your nose."

She glared at him. "I like my nose." They turned a corner and stepped into another street. There were knots of people gathered here and there and no one seemed to be paying attention to Tomiko. "I do not see our last attacker." *Does Saris truly have agents everywhere?* "We must be more cautious."

"We should split up."

"You still think that?"

"I do. For the honour of my clan, I must stop her."

"What foolishness is honour?" she scoffed. "It will only see you dead in the street."

"I cannot live without honour," he replied.

I am not sure that I can live without you, she thought. And wondered from where such a thought had come.

Chapter Eight

Morning came and Tomiko entered the main room of her home to find Yoshitsune kneeling in *seiza-* fashion near the low table, gathering up his possessions.

"Getting an early start on the day?" she asked him. Her bare feet enjoyed the warmth of the floor—and the lack of confining shoes. The sun was shining through the open window and warming the room nicely.

"After we parted company yesterday, I wandered for some time."

Tomiko nodded. She had returned to her home alone after their disagreement. "I did not hear you enter."

"You were sleeping and I took care to be quiet." Yoshitsune paused to stare at a small pebble he had placed on the tabletop. "I spoke at length with one of Shinzu's friends last night."

"Oh?"

"We met near the start of the *Tokaido* highway, in the Yoshiwara District." He blushed at the mention of Edo's red light district. "He told me that barges bearing the *mon* of Lady Saris often sail along the Chiba to Edo." Shinzu had described the *mon* to them before his death: two jade squiggles against a yellow field. "She has a stronghold somewhere to the north of the capitol."

"You learned much last night." Tomiko frowned. *And after we spent a week hunting for rumours on our own.*

"Shinzu had many friends. They seek vengeance for his death."

"Rumours in the streets and markets say that the poet died of a seizure in his bed."

Yoshitsune frowned. "That's a lie."

"You and I know that. The rest of Edo does not. Someone is working to keep the existence of the Cult a secret from all others." Tomiko tapped her fingers on the table. "Two sets of assassins have been set upon us. We leave their bodies in the streets. Shinzu is murdered in a tavern and yet no talk of this has reached the streets of Edo."

"The city thrives on gossip."

"Yes, it does." Normally gossip and rumour moved as swift as the deed occurred. "There is a powerful personage attempting to block the truth."

"Saris Taira?"

Tomiko tilted her head to the left, a very bird-like gesture. "She would be my first guess."

"Only your first?"

"Shogun Tokugawa, or members of his court, might also be working to suppress knowledge of the Cult for their own reasons. They could be working with the *Naga* or plotting to take advantage of Saris's scheming for their own advancement."

Yoshitsune shook his head. "It is growing so complicated."

"Life in the capitol is not the same as life in a farming village. The Daimyos plot and scheme with and against the Shogun. All plot for family and the increasing status of their families. The Tokugawas are plotting just as much as everyone else." Tomiko reached for a ripe persimmon. Yoshitsune had an assortment of fruits arranged on the table. "Where did this come from?"

"I found a *bote-uri* this morning while I was out."

"Did you plan to leave without saying good-bye?"

"No," he replied quickly. "I offer you this fruit in exchange for all your help. I know that it is hardly equal to what I owe you, but it is all I can offer you right now."

"I did not think you had any coin."

He blushed. "Shinzu had many friends here in Edo...so do I." He tapped the pouch at his *obi*. It was more rounded than Tomiko was used to seeing. "I can offer you more."

"There is no need of repayment." She paused, unsure what else to say. "Your company has been most welcome. This house has been far too empty of late."

Yoshitsune looked uncomfortable. "I must leave you though. I must travel to the north in search of the estate home to Lady Saris."

"And there you will seek vengeance?"

"I must. Saris must answer for her crimes."

"There is a bitter truth in your words." Tomiko watched him finish packing up his few possessions. "You leave me with little choice, Yoshitsune, other than to help you in this quest of yours."

He looked at her.

"*We* will journey north, but not in search of the estates of Lady Saris. No, first we must visit another stronghold." She sounded resigned to that, but there was a certain wistfulness in her voice. "I will see that you are properly trained in the arts of the sword. If you are to succeed, then you will need much training and a new blade." She gestured to the knife at his waist. "One small *tanto*, however fine its lineage, will not suffice."

"You are a very wise woman."

"Thank you. Age does bring wisdom...if the young will listen."

"*Young*?" he asked. "I have seen twenty-three summers," he boasted.

Tomiko laughed at him. "I have seen over three *hundred* and twenty-three summers."

Yoshitsune blinked.

"Time passes differently for my kind." She smiled at his confusion. "Come, we must prepare for our journey."

* * *

"If we are to go north, why do we leave Edo on the *Tokaido*?"

"We go southwest because I wish to travel so." She walked along the street at a steady pace that would carry her quickly along the road at a speed she could maintain for hours. *Even with these damned shoes on my feet.* The pack on her back was relatively small. *It is best to travel light.* "The *Tokaido* goes south. Our foe waits to the north. If *Naga* are watching for us, and I would not tempt the gods by assuming otherwise, they will likely not think to guard the south gate as they would the north."

"We are wasting our time." Yoshitsune had been grumbling since they entered the Takanawa district. The area was characterized by tightly packed row houses, workshops, stores, and official buildings. The streets bustled with people.

"It is only a little extra time. We can spare it easily." She smiled and gestured with her right hand. "There is the official gate."

Yoshitsune stared at the broad, imposing stone wall that crossed the main road. He knew that the wall was part of the fortifications designed to protect the city from enemies. "So that is the *Takanawa Okido*," he said.

"Yes, that is the great wooden gate."

"I entered Edo through the *Yotsuya Okido*."

She nodded. "Both gates mark the boundaries of the city."

There were many people milling around the district. The square near the gate was the place where relatives and friends traditionally said their farewells to people traveling west from Edo. It seemed that there would be many people setting out on journeys this morning.

"We have no one to wish us luck and speed on the road," Tomiko noted sadly.

"I am surprised that Yori did not come to see you off."

"She is far too frail to journey this far."

"Did you tell her you were leaving?"

"No, I did not. I left a note." Tomiko wondered if she should have made the effort to say good-bye in person. *Yori, Saito, Yasuki...there are many who will miss me when I leave Edo and not return.*

* * *

The western road was not overly busy. There were only a few other travelers in sight as they walked. Most of those they saw were merchants, with guards; the rest were simple farmers.

Towards noon, Tomiko and Yoshitsune walked past one of the Shogun's estates.

"Perhaps we shall see Ieyasu out hawking." Yoshitsune looked over his shoulder towards the half-glimpsed plume of smoke from the kitchen fires.

"Perhaps."

"I have never seen the shogun."

"Most of us haven't." Tomiko offered him a shrug. "He is an important man, with many concerns upon his time. He would have little time to waste speaking with us."

"We could warn him of the *Naga*."

"He might not believe us. We have no proof of their plotting." Tomiko rubbed at the side of her nose. *He will need firm proof before he dares move any of his soldiers away from the capitol. True proof before he risks starting a war.*

"We know of Saris."

"What do we truly know of her?"

"That she sent assassins after us. After me at least," Yoshitsune amended quickly. "She killed Shinzu and probably the others who whispered their rumours to him. We know that she plots on behalf of the Naga."

"But we have no proof aside from her name."

"Saris Taira has a stronghold."

"Yes, *somewhere north of Edo*. We do not its precise location, or even if it truly exists. The shogun will not listen to us without solid proof of her treason."

Yoshitsune grumbled, but made no further argument.

They passed a road marker.

"How far have we come?"

"Not far enough." Tomiko squinted at the marker. "Tokugawa Ieyasu uses the Nihonbashi bridge as the zero point for his network of roads. We have come a mere twelve kilometres so far."

"I thought that we were making good time."

"We are, though we would travel faster by horse."

"Only samurai and nobles travel by horse," he replied in surprise. "Do you have such aspirations?"

"Everyone has aspirations, Yoshitsune. But I do not wish to be mistaken for one of the nobility." *It might lead to awkward questions later.* "You are correct...we are making acceptable time for our journey. If time truly pressed upon us..." her voice trailed away into silence.

"If time pressed?" Yoshitsune repeated. "Then what?"

"Then we might seek...alternate transportation." She smiled warmly at his confused expression. "But we are not yet pressed so we shall leave that option. All right?"

Yoshitsune nodded. "All right," he agreed, even though his face and tone betrayed his confusion.

Tomiko nodded to herself as they continued walking.

Chapter Nine

"Alms?" the old woman asked in a piteous tone from where she crouched amid the gnarled roots of a pine tree. Her face was hidden beneath her hat and her hands clenched her skirts tightly. "Alms for the sick, good sir?"

"Of course, good mother." Yoshitsune reached for his purse while Tomiko looked back over her shoulder at the otherwise deserted road. "You have a lonely vigil on this stretch of road."

"There has been little traffic all day," the old woman agreed.

"There is little around here." Tomiko studied the drooping pine branches. Some half smelled scent tickled at her nose. "Is your home close by?" *Surely she did not walk very far.*

"Close enough, good mistress."

"A lonely road," Yoshitsune commented as he removed some coins from his purse. "You are lucky to not be accosted by bandits."

"The Shogun's guards patrol it often enough. Bandits do not bother an old woman like myself. What have I to steal?" She chuckled in a gurgling manner.

"What indeed." Tomiko looked around again. "It is such a lonely place." That odd scent plagued her.

"I like the solitude." The old woman kept her face down, staring at the hard-packed dirt of the road. "There's quite a nice hot spring not far from here where I can soak away my body's ills."

"There's nothing quite like a good relaxing soak," Tomiko agreed, rubbing at her nose. "Perhaps on the return journey I should seek out this hot spring of yours."

"You might enjoy it." The old woman gurgled her laughter again. "Thank you, young man. The Gods will bless you for such kindness." She held out a shaking hand towards him. "Closer, that I might thank you for your kindness."

Yoshitsune took a step closer.

"She's not sick," Tomiko warned him. "She does not smell sick."

The old woman snarled and lunged to her feet with surprising swiftness. She gave a peculiar hissing cry as she flung herself at Yoshitsune.

He fumbled his dagger free of his *obi* just as the woman crashed into his body. The two tumbled onto the dusty roadway and rolled.

"Yoshitsune!" Tomiko grabbed the old woman's shoulder and flung her aside. "Are you all right?"

"Yes," he gasped. Blinking, he quickly scrambled back to his feet. "What of her?"

The old woman was laying in a heap on the ground, where Tomiko had roughly thrown her.

"We have questions that you would be wise to answer for us!" Tomiko grasped her shoulder and rolled her over.

Yoshitsune's *tanto* was embedded in her heart.

The young man stared at the corpse. "I killed her!"

"Yes." Tomiko nodded.

"I am dishonoured!" he wailed. "I have slain a defenceless old grandmother." He fell to his knees in the dirt. "There is no redemption possible for such an act!"

"Spare me these protestations about your precious honour." Tomiko pulled the dagger from the corpse's breast and wiped it clean on the old woman's sleeve. "She tried to kill you."

"She was sick…deranged. She could not help herself."

"She has fangs."

"What?" Yoshitsune bent closer to look. "Are those *scales* on her neck?"

"And she bled green blood, not red." Tomiko gestured to the stains on the woman's sleeve. "She is another *Naga*."

"They're still hunting us?"

Tomiko looked around. The road was still quite deserted. "Yes, it would appear so."

"By the Gods."

Tomiko looked around. "A lonely place for a traveller or two to disappear. And a nice hot spring nearby to wash up in afterwards."

"And little risk of the Shogun's patrols stumbling across you while you hide the bodies." Yoshitsune nodded. "A good trap indeed."

* * *

"Are you certain we are traveling the right path?"

"I am."

"You seem nervous."

"I'm not." Tomiko paused to stretch out her aching back, sore from carrying her pack for so long. "I am just not used to walking for days and days along the roads. It has been a long time since I last travelled such a distance."

"You have done well," Yoshitsune told her. He paused a moment to try and unsuccessfully brush some of the dust of the road from his pants.

Tomiko frowned as she studied the landmarks. *What landmarks I can see through such thick forest.* "Finally." She gestured towards a particularly twisted pine tree. "We approach the shrine I seek." The main road was far behind them now. There were no markers on this overgrown path, a hundred kilometres or more from Edo. "We will rest there for the night."

"A shrine?" Yoshitsune shook his head as he followed her. "This entire place is like a dream." The trees were twisted into strange shapes, almost as if they were in pain. The ground beyond the narrow path was moist, with many ponds and bogs. A pale mist hung low over the ground, curling around the tree trunks and obscuring the exposed roots. "Are we safe?"

"We will be safe enough." Tomiko had cast aside her usual disguise, walking along the path with unshod feet and allowing the breeze to tug at her hair and feathery cloak. She knew there was little risk of meeting other travellers on this path. "The Naga should not know of this shrine's location and it has certain...protections." Or so she hoped.

Yoshitsune frowned. "Will the protections endanger us?"

"Of course not."

"I'm thirsty."

"As am I." Tomiko waved her hand. "There is good water nearby. A spring-fed pond so clear that you can see the fish at the very bottom. I often think that it is the best water in all of Japan. It lays just ahead."

"Lead me to it." Yoshitsune smiled eagerly.

The pond came into view through the bushes.

"It looks wholesome enough."

Tomiko nodded. "It is perfectly safe to drink. We can refill our water skins there."

Laughter echoed through the trees.

They both froze in mid-step.

Yoshitsune rested his hand on his small dagger. He looked around, but saw no one. He assumed a stance of prepared alertness, ready to throw himself at whatever threat might appear.

Tomiko laid her hand on his shoulder. "It's all right."

"Are we near the shrine then?" Yoshitsune continued to stare into the trees. "Is that one of the protectors?"

"Yes."

More laughter echoed from among the mist-shrouded trees. "You have brought me a snack, Tomiko-san. How kind of you!"

Yoshitsune flinched as the reedy voice boomed out from among the trees. He gripped the bared *tanto* more tightly in his fist, but didn't draw it.

Tomiko shook her head. "I have brought you a student!"

"Looks more like a snack to me." The creature dropped from a tree branch and cackled loudly as it landed on the ground. "A tasty snack." A wide smile split his monkey-like face, under a long beak-like nose. His slimy skin had a peculiar yellow-green colouration, and the tortoise-shell on his back was a mottled blue-green.

Yoshitsune eyed the monkey-like creature, resting his hand on his *tanto*. Despite it only being the size of a ten-year-old child, he knew how dangerous it would be. "He is *Kappa*."

Tomiko nodded calmly. She did not appear to be frightened in the least. "Yes, Yoshitsune, he is indeed."

The *Kappa* spread his webbed hands and feet, taking up a wrestler's stance. "Is your new pet ready to face me?" He wore a ragged brown kimono and *geta* on his feet.

"I am no one's pet!"

The *Kappa* cackled maliciously in that off-putting reedy voice. "So you claim." His laughter stilled and he assumed a wrestler's stance. "Prove it," he snarled.

Yoshitsune offered the tortoise-shelled demon a polite, and deep, bow.

The *Kappa* returned it immediately. Water splashed from the bowl-like depression atop its head. It hastily straightened upright with a curse.

Tomiko smiled.

The *Kappa* whirled to face her. "Damn you, Tomiko! You taught him too well."

"I can take no credit for this, Kisho. He learned the secrets of your kind's power at his grandmother's fire." Bow to a *Kappa* and he would bow in return, thus spilling out the water that gave him his strength.

"Do you still wish to wrestle?" Yoshitsune demanded.

The *Kappa* looked at him and then threw back his head and laughed. "He has spirit at least. Maybe I won't eat him."

"You can try to eat me...I will give you such stomach cramps that you will vomit up all that you have eaten for the last year."

"You think that you can defeat me, boy?"

"*Kappa no kawa nagare.*"

The *Kappa* looked surprised for a long moment, then laughed a deep belly laugh. "Yes, *even Kappas* can drown," he agreed with a nod. He turned to the *Tengu*. "If I am not to eat this boy, why bring him here?"

"We seek your aid in a quest," Yoshitsune answered for her.

Kisho shook his head, and then he shook it again when he turned to look at her. "I am not fighting for him, Tomiko. I will not leave my home." He gestured to the bogs that surrounded them. "These are my home waters. I will defend them from all who trespass, but I will not venture forth to fight needlessly."

"The Emperor is grave danger."

"He is *your* emperor, human, not *mine*."

"The capitol faces equal danger. The lives of thousands are at risk."

"Again, it is *your* capitol, Yoshitsune. What are the lives of thousands of humans to me?"

"You have your own problems then, Kisho?" Tomiko asked.

"*Naga*," he spat. "They have been draining water from the streams for some time. Many of my favourite ponds along the Chiba have been polluted."

"Polluted?"

"Poisoned." Kisho spat again. "Poison is a favoured ploy by the *Naga*. What else do you expect from snakes?"

Yoshitsune frowned. "Could they plot to poison Edo?"

"Possibly," Tomiko admitted. "It would be a tactically wise move on their part. Poison the city's cisterns and Saris could kill off hundreds in a single day. All of Edo would be thrown into a panic by such widespread death."

Kisho was listening closely. "They have a stronghold nearby. An old ruin they have inhabited and rebuilt. Some fool Human noble has a flag flying over the place now. I have never ventured too close, but a few wandering *Naga* have learned to respect the waters around the ruins."

The monkey-like features of his face gave him a truly sinister expression as he said that. "I do not keep track of the petty titles Humans give themselves, but the *mon* on the banner is of two squiggles of jade against a golden field."

Yoshitsune's brown eyes widened. "Lady Saris."

"*Saris*?" the *Kappa* hissed. "Saris Taira?"

"That is a name we have heard."

"So it is *she*." Kisho frowned, and his monkey-like features actually looked worried. "She is dangerous, Tomiko. Very dangerous." His voice had dropped into a whisper. "She is old too, far older than any of these humans."

"How old can she be? Shinzu told us she's been plotting and scheming since the rise of the Shogunate."

The *Kappa* laughed. "For a mere fifty years?" he asked. "You think she is some old grandmother who schemes by the winter fires?"

"No, I don't—"

"Foolish boy, Saris has been plotting her revenge ever since your first emperor overthrew her kind." He cackled at Yoshitsune's startled expression. "You've had what, a hundred and ten emperors?" He cackled again and then turned to face Tomiko, still laughing at the human's expression. "The boy truly has no idea what he is up against!"

"What *we* are up against. He has my help."

Startled into silence, the *Kappa* eyed her warily.

Tomiko stared back at him. "Don't you think that is enough?"

"Hardly." Kisho shook his head and brushed his black hair away from his face.

"Well, I am all that he has."

"You are growing more foolish with age," Kisho told her bluntly. "Or are you suffering from some disease?" His orange eyes narrowed, then abruptly they grew wide. "Perhaps you have fallen in—"

"My reason are my own," she interrupted. "Can you help us?"

"I cannot leave my home waters. You know that."

Yoshitsune frowned. "Then we have wasted our time on this journey."

"No journey is ever wasted." Tomiko paused as she looked at him, then back at the leering *Kappa*. "We have learned more than we knew before and knowledge of our foe is vital if we are triumph over her. You have my thanks, Kisho, for telling us what you could of Saris."

"I listen to the voices on the wind," the *Kappa* replied. "A little bird told me that you might be venturing away from your nest."

Tomiko frowned.

"I wish that I could help you more, but I do not travel far from my home." Kisho gestured to the surrounding bog. "I can tell you that Saris has made enemies over the years. A great number of them. You will find other allies who can help you." He waved his hand towards Yoshitsune. "Someone to teach this whelp how to fight with a sword perhaps?"

"First I *need* a sword with which to fight."

"That could be arranged." Kisho chuckled. "If Tomiko can bend her pride enough to accept *his* welcome home."

Now it was Tomiko's eyes that went wide. "Is *he* still alive?"

"Of course."

She took a deep breath. "Where?"

"Up on Mount Kurama. In his usual place of course." Kisho paused, studying her face. "He'll be waiting for you."

Tomiko turned away. "I'm not sure we should bother him."

"You would bother me for aid, but then avoid one of your own flock?" Kisho snorted. "You *are* growing foolish with age Tomiko-*san*. He misses you."

Tomiko stood silently, her eyes misted over with memory and thought.

"He can teach the boy how to fight like a master swordsman."

Yoshitsune perked up at that. "Who can?"

"Tomiko's—"

"No one of importance."

"Have it your way then." Kisho was smiling widely at her interruption. "You need help, Tomiko, you told me that yourself. He knows all about your current problems. Most of us do by now."

"How?"

"Oh, a little bird told us."

She frowned. "*Benkei.*"

Kisho shrugged in response.

"I don't need him to interfere!"

"You do need help though. Saris worships Naga Padoha."

Yoshitsune frowned in confusion. "Who?"

Kisho spat. "The serpent ruler of *Yomi.*"

"The Corpse Queen of the Underworld?" Yoshitsune shivered at the thought of facing such a demon. "Dear Gods protect us."

"At least we are not facing Her." The *Kappa* shook his head carefully. "From what I have heard, the *Naga* serve this Lady Saris. They are turning the banks of the Chiba into a virtual replica of Yomi, the land of filth."

"We plan to stop her."

"You have set yourselves a difficult task...I wish you success in it." The *Kappa* abruptly whirled and a *shuriken* flashed from his webbed fingers.

Coiled about a branch, an adder was transfixed by the weapon.

"Damnable creatures are everywhere." The *Kappa* giggled.

Chapter Ten

The dirt path dipped down somewhat, cutting around large and weatherworn boulders. The mountains towered above the two travellers, the path vanishing into the distance, lost in mist and pines and boulders.

"Where are we?"

"On the slopes of Mount Kurama."

Yoshitsune sighed at Tomiko's calm matter-of-fact answer. The subtle humour was what he had expected to hear from her. "I know that much...I hope that we might be near some village. A shrine even."

"No humans dwell this high up the mountain's sides. It is pristine wilderness here." She inhaled deeply. "The mountain air is very rich and enjoyable, is it not?"

"It is potent with the pines." Yoshitsune breathed deeply, trying to catch his breath. "You set a hard pace for us."

"We have much distance to travel and little time." Tomiko was breathing somewhat more heavily than normal as well. "Perhaps I push myself more than I think."

"You are not young," Yoshitsune reminded her.

"I am not some crippled grandmother either, who hobbles only as far as her futon."

"I meant no disrespect." Yoshitsune hastily bowed towards her. "I merely meant that we had both travelled far on this journey and neither of us is used to such distance." He lifted his head and gazed towards the mountain's still-distant peak. "We are a very long way from Edo."

"Nearly three hundred kilometres."

"My feet feel every step, as yours surely must," he added. "We could have taken a ship in Edo and sailed almost to here."

"I did not intend for us to come *here*," Tomiko admitted in a soft voice. "I did not truly know what our destination would be when we set out from Edo. I had thoughts and suspicions, but I did not truly know whence our path would lead." She sighed. "It has led us here," she whispered. "Little though did I wish to come." She paused, then spoke in a louder tone. "We are almost at our journey's end."

"You do not sound excited by that prospect." Yoshitsune shook his head as he trudged wearily alongside his companion as they continued to climb the mountain. "You said that yesterday...and the day before. I feel lost."

"We are not lost. We are making good time for our journey." Tomiko picked her steps carefully through the rocks and boulders that dictated the pathway's winding course. Pine trees grew thickly on the slopes, a near solid wall of foliage forcing them to keep to a single path. "If Kisho was right," she added somewhat reluctantly, "then we have no other choice left to us but to journey here."

"And where is here? You still haven't told me where we are going. Other than a mountain top."

"We travel to a place of refuge...I hope."

The young man stopped walking for a moment, and to stare at his companion with a concerned expression on his face. "This is one of the few times that you have not been certain of yourself," he said.

Tomiko didn't reply.

With a sigh, the human resumed walking. "Surely you do not mean to climb to the very top of the peak?"

"We shall climb as high as necessary." Tomiko maintained a steady pace. Her bare feet found sufficient purchase and she was in no danger of slipping. *It was easier traveling here the last time. So much easier just to take wing and...* She shook her head to clear it of such thoughts. *That time is long past*, she reminded herself. She heard Yoshitsune stumble as loose rocks shifted under his feet.

"The footing is treacherous." Yoshitsune regained his footing and his balance. "One misstep and you could slide right back to the bottom."

"Yes, you easily could" Tomiko answered absently. "He does not appreciate outsiders disturbing him."

"No, *I* do not." A tall, crow-headed *Tengu* with long white hair in place of feathers dropped out of the tree and landed on the ground with a soft crunch of his talons sinking into the gravel. "What do you have there, Tomiko?" he demanded. He was a head taller than Yoshitsune and had pale green feathers on his face and on his arms.

"*Konichi-wa*, Sojobo." She carefully offered him a deep and respectful bow.

"*Konichi-wa*," he replied, returning a shallow bow of his own. "I had not expected to see *you* in this place."

"I felt that we had little choice but to come."

Yoshitsune stared at the *Tengu's* ears, just visible on the sides of his head amidst his feathers and long white hair.

Sojobo's stubby beak opened just enough to show his sharp fangs. "Little choice indeed if it has led *you* back to my nest."

Tomiko stared at him, then looked down at her dusty feet.

He clasped his hands in front of his kimono-clad chest and clicked his beak twice. "Speak openly and do not waste my time."

"We seek allies against Lady Saris!" Yoshitsune burst out. He glanced towards his companion, but Tomiko remained silent.

"The leader of the *Naga*?"

"You have heard of them?"

Sojobo nodded. "Everyone in our clan has heard of them by now." His claw-tipped right hand was holding a *shakujo*, with rings tied to the top of the wooden staff. His grip tightened enough on it that his knuckles went white.

"Can you help us?" Yoshitsune asked politely.

"I *can*, I *could*…but *will* I?" Sojobo chuckled softly at the young human's confusion. "Why should I?"

"Because the fate of the Shogunate is at stake."

Sojobo shook his head slowly. "The affairs of humans are of little concern to us. We dwell beyond the human realm, without allegiance to your Emperor or his Shogun." He turned his head. "Tomiko, you should have known better than to bring a man-child here."

She stirred at that. "The *Naga* are plotting against all of us...or so Benkei told me. Was he lying to me?"

"Benkei has never lied to anyone. If anything, he takes great pleasure in sharing uncomfortable truths with people."

Yoshitsune took a step closer to the *Tengu sensei*. The red skin of Sojobo's arms and legs made an interesting contrast to his green feathers. "You must aid us. I, Minamoto Yoshitsune, will pledge my honour and my life to you in return for whatever aid you can provide to us."

The *Tengu* tilted his head to the left and studied him anew. "An interesting offer."

Laughter sounded from among the trees.

Yoshitsune looked up startled. A dozen *Tengu* were watching from where they perched among the pine branches. Their feathers were either green or black, but they all had the wrinkled red skin of their kind.

Tomiko was the most Human-looking of the lot.

"He makes this bargain rashly and without much forethought, eh Tomiko? I could offer you both a simple meal and a warm fire for the night as my *aid* to you, and then you would be bound by this bargain."

Yoshitsune shook his head. "You are *karasu Tengu*. I trust you to act with due honour."

Sojobo clicked his beak again, and his brown eyes narrowed. "What do you want me to do with him, Tomiko?" he asked.

"Train him." Tomiko stepped closer to the other *Tengu*. "He has talent...I have seen him fight and he shows much promise. With the proper training, at the hands of a master, he will be a worthy foe of the *Naga*."

"Flattery from you?"

"Truth."

Sojobo nodded with some reluctance. "You lie as seldom as Benkei," he muttered. He turned his head. "Prepare the practice grounds. Fetch this boy a practice blade and let him prove his supposed worth to us all."

"Yes, *Sensei*." A black-feathered *Tengu* fluttered away into the trees.

"We shall prepare ourselves." Sojobo offered them a bow, then turned, and jumped impossibly high into the air. He vanished into the treetops.

"I thought the other *Tengu* weren't going to help you?" Yoshitsune looked at her, tilting his head to the side.

Almost bird-like, she thought in amusement. "He was my *Sensei*," she replied soberly. "He will help us now." She continued to walk along the pathway. "Come quickly, he will not enjoy waiting for you."

The path opened into a clearing. Mount Kurama itself continued to climb towards the clouds, but here there was a clearing of fairly large proportions, a canyon walled with rock on three sides and trees on the last. A waterfall fell along the western wall and a stream meandered through the valley before vanishing among the trees. Caves had been dug into the mountainside and their mouths gaped open. Several dozen huts, raised up on stilts, stood in eight groups, set throughout the clearing.

Tomiko gazed at the scene with a loud sigh of contentment. "The sights and smells of home," she said aloud. *There are more huts than I remember...the Clan must have grown.* The cherry trees clustered along the eastern slope of the mountain were lush and scented the air heavily with their blossoms.

"I feel so out of place here." Yoshitsune looked around with some nervousness. The cheery trees looked almost ready to flower, despite the fact that summer was rapidly passing into fall. He let his pack drop onto the grass.

Dozens of *Tengu* were gathering in groups, watching him with open curiosity. Other *Tengu* were emerging from the huts and calling to each other with bird-like whistles.

"You are safe enough among them—er, us." Tomiko rested her hand on his shoulder, feeling her cheeks grow hot with blood.

Yoshitsune looked at her with complete trust.

"I brought you here as my guest...you will not be harmed. At least not deliberately," Tomiko hastily amended as Sojobo emerged from one of the caves, followed by a black-headed *Tengu* who was carrying two bamboo swords.

The tall green *Tengu* stepped closer to his guests and studied them both. "We shall use *shinei*."

Yoshitsune took one of the practice swords from the other *Tengu* and hastily examined it. It was as he expected—a bundle of thin bamboo sticks, loosely bound with twine. He knew, from past experience, that it would make a loud *clack* and leave a welt whenever it struck flesh. He gave it a swing to see just how it felt in his hand. "It is well-balanced."

"Of course it is. I do not practice with faulty weapons." The *Tengu* paused a moment in silent approval as he watched the young human continue to test the sword's balance. "Do you wish *do* or *men* or a *kabuto*?"

Yoshitsune quickly shook his head. "I am comfortable without such play-armour, if you are."

"I do wish for my *kabuto*." Another *Tengu* hurried forward with a helmet that Sojobo hastily plunked atop his feathered head. "Let us begin."

The two combatants bowed politely to one another. Each man straightened and they studied each other, neither willing to make the first move.

Sojobo paused a moment longer, then erupted into motion, his feather-covered cloak swirling around him like giant wings.

The practice blades flashed and struck against each other as Yoshitsune desperately blocked the swing. The clatter of the bamboo striking against each other filled the clearing as the two fought.

Tomiko watched with a critical eye as the two swordsmen traded blows. Yoshitsune was at a disadvantage—that much was obvious from the first slash. It was all that he could do to turn aside Sojobo's blows and keep the *Tengu's* strikes from reaching him.

Other *Tengu* had gathered to watch the impromptu duel. Several whistled their amusement at the display. A few did comment on how much effort Yoshitsune was making.

But it won't be enough to win, Tomiko thought. *He's far too untrained to be able to match Sojobo.* Not that she had expected anything less to come of this. *He must prove his own worth, else there is no hope.*

Sojobo paused for a moment, and then took a deep breath before bursting into movement. He thrust his blade in a lightning fast series of sweeping blows that forced the human to retreat step by step.

Then Yoshitsune ducked one sweep and threw himself into the attack. His own wooden blade passed so by Sojobo's arm so closely that his feathers parted by the wind of the swing.

Sojobo looked startled, and then his brown eyes narrowed. His own defensive swings remained controlled, but they gained both speed and intensity.

Then his burst of energy was seemingly spent and Yoshitsune fell back, panting.

Sojobo gave one final flurry of motion and his *shinei* struck Yoshitsune's arm.

Yoshitsune dropped his sword, more from startlement than from pain.

"And it ends." Sojobo held his practice sword an inch from Yoshitsune's neck.

The young man bowed deeply. He was panting. "So it does, *sensei*."

Sojobo accepted a mug of water from one of his other students and took a long swallow. "The human fights well enough, Tomiko."

"*Domo arigato*."

Yoshitsune wiped his face with the sleeve of his *haori*. A blue-feathered *Tengu* brought him water in a clay mug.

"Of course," Sojobo added, "any hatchling could have defeated you. I was simply being nice."

Yoshitsune's eyes narrowed and he handed his own now-empty mug of water back to the *Tengu* who had given it to him. "Perhaps I was merely showing some respect to my honoured *elders*." He picked his *shinei* up off the ground and assumed a battle ready stance.

"*So ka?* Show proper respect by giving me your full display of martial prowess then!" He lunged himself at Yoshitsune who blocked the blow.

Tomiko shook her head as they began to dance once again. "Men!" she snorted.

Chapter Eleven

Throughout the clearing, *Tengu* fought with both *shinei* and with real swords.

"I have trained students in the arts of swordsmanship for nearly five hundred years," Sojobo announced in a calm voice. He was kneeling, *seiza*-style, on a small dais, watching his students train. "In all that time, I have taught fewer than twenty humans. Most of them proved only to be severe disappointments to my teaching."

Yoshitsune carefully poured his *sensei* a mug of *sake*. He handed it over, and then moved to kneel a few paces away from the old *Tengu*. He remained silent, as befitted his place as an aspiring student.

Sojobo never looked around, though he sipped his sake. "The *Tengu* practice as I require. They master the arts of the sword as I teach them. Can a man-child show patience enough to match them?"

Yoshitsune said nothing, but kept his eyes downcast.

"You fight well enough...and you learn quickly in your lessons. If you are able to master all the skills which I seek to impart, then you might yet realize your potential to become the greatest swordsman in all of Japan." The elderly *Tengu* chuckled at Yoshitsune's startled expression. "Greatest *Human* swordsman, that is."

Yoshitsune licked his lips. "A worthy goal, *Sensei*, but I do not seek to become the greatest swordsman in all of Japan."

"*So ka?*" Sojobo did not hide his surprise at that denial. "I train all of my students to aspire to such greatness."

"I will be humbly content with exacting vengeance upon the *Naga*."

"There is more to life than merely exacting vengeance, Yoshitsune. You will learn that in time I trust." Sojobo gestured towards the training sessions with his right hand while he lifted his mug of sake with his left. "You *do* have much to learn."

* * *

"Are there many *Tengu* clans?"

"Yes." Tomiko picked a dried plum from the dish and settled back into the lush grass that grew near the stream. *Nothing wrong with a picnic lunch under a mostly clear sky,* she thought. *It is good to get away from the others for a time.* "Not all of them are represented here." Wind rustled through the pine trees and carried their strong scent to her. "Most of them are scattered amongst the mountains and forests of Japan."

"I see." He was the only human in the camp, although none of the *Tengu* made mention of that fact or treated him any differently than they did each other. "Sojobo is an important man."

"Yes, he is the head of one of the most influential Clans."

"You don't seem comfortable here."

Tomiko looked at him. "Why do you say that?" she asked. *Mmm, he looks even more filled out.* His kimono was hanging partially open and his arms were bared. *Practice with the sword is doing him much good.*

"You don't look at ease." Yoshitsune swallowed a cherry. "I would have thought you would be happy to be back among your own kind."

"I was happy in Edo."

"But not here?"

"I am *Tengu.* My people are *Tengu.*" She gestured towards the surrounding mountains. "We are people of the mountains and forests. We live among wild things."

"Yet you chose to live in the capitol, amongst humans."

"Yes."

A crow cawed from somewhere in a nearby pine.

"I was not happy here..."

"Yet you were happy in Edo."

"At times, yes. Are *you* happy here?"

"I am learning so much." Yoshitsune stared up at the passing clouds. "Sojobo *sensei* works me hard, but no harder than he works any other student. I'm learning skills and forms that no other man knows!"

"You will be a great swordsman."

"*Hai*," he agreed.

"But will you meet your fate in such a duel?"

"I am not some foolish child, Tomiko. I am not going to swagger around the streets of Edo picking fights with other samurai simply to prove my prowess."

"I should hope not," a new voice interrupted. "Such behaviour would gravely dishonour Sojobo's teachings."

Tomiko's head turned. "Benkei!" she exclaimed.

The crow-headed *Tengu* dropped out of a pine tree and bowed his green-feathered head politely towards her. "Tomiko-sama."

"I had thought to see you here before this."

"This is *my* home," the crow-headed *Tengu* agreed. "Far away from the crowded and noisy humans." He clicked his beak. "Well, *most* of them."

"Have you any interesting news to share with us?"

"About your pet humans? Or about the scheming of Lady Saris?"

Yoshitsune gazed back at him blandly, as if he was not listening to the veiled insults.

Benkei clicked his beak once, clearly surprised that the young man was not rising to the bait he was dangling.

"Either would do for now."

Yoshitsune stared at other *Tengu*. "What is Saris doing?"

"I have no idea. The Cult is being very quiet right now." Benkei cawed with amused laughter. "A quiet cult is never a good thing I suspect."

Tomiko nodded her head. "Saris must be planning to move soon."

Yoshitsune scrambled to his feet. "We're wasting time here."

"The time spent here is not being wasted!" Tomiko told him sternly. "You cannot face the Cult before you are ready. They would kill you in an instant."

Yoshitsune slumped back onto the grass.

"The *Naga* are far more dangerous than even Sojobo gives them credit for being." Benkei shook his head slowly. "This affair will not end well, Tomiko."

"It will end as it must."

"A simple enough statement." Benkei shook his head. "Do you place yourself into the hands of uncaring fate? Or will you seek to fly your own course?"

"We do what we must. Fate led us to Mount Kurama and Sojobo."

"You must have some interesting karma if you were able to convince Sojobo to train your pet human, Tomiko. I seem to recall you saying, once upon a time, that you would not return to this place."

"Times change. Everyone says things they later regret."

Benkei laughed. "How true."

* * *

Tomiko nibbled at one of the rice cakes she had taken from a beaten-copper platter that was being passed around the cavern. *Not as good as the ones Yori-sama shared with me*, she thought sadly. The other Tengu were eating and drinking, gathering in small groups scattered around the cavern and the central fire pit. *Yoshitsune is the only human here. Likely the only human around within days and days of walking. Yet he does not complain, merely pushes himself to work harder and match the* Tengu *he trains with.*

Sojobo sipped at the silver goblet of plum wine that he held in one of his claw-tipped hands. In the other, he carried a fan made from seven feathers which acted as a sign of his position at the top of *Tengu* society "Your skills increase, Yoshitsune. Would that some of my own *Tengu* had your dedication to mastering the arts of the sword."

"I am nothing without the guidance of my *sensei's* teachings." Yoshitsune kept his voice polite and neutral. He wore a plain blue kimono and his black hair and bare face seemed out of place amongst the feathers and plumage of the *Tengu*.

A distant rumble of thunder shook the cavern.

"You are entering a most dangerous time…you feel the call of your skills and yet you are not yet a master."

"I fought before I came to this place. I will fight again when I leave it."

"Yes, but the foes you face are more than mortal. The *Naga* are very dangerous foes indeed. Granted, the Purebloods are no more fearsome than any normal Humans, given slightly better agility and reflexes, but they are still the offspring of serpents and have all the speed and deadly skills of the snakes they worship."

"I have faced *Naga* in battle before."

"So Tomiko has told me." Sojobo frowned, and then he shook his head. "Yet you have only faced Purebloods."

Yoshitsune frowned. "Purebloods? You keep using that name, but it means little to me."

Sojobo settled back on his haunches. "There are various breeds of *Naga,* subspecies, if you will. All are *Naga,* but three bloodlines are distinctly seen."

The fire was crackling brightly and its light and warmth kept the cavern warm. Many *Tengu* had gathered there over the course of the evening, and now they fell silent as they listened quietly to his story.

Sojobo eyed the gathered clan and he pitched his voice to carry to everyone. "Once, in a past now shrouded by long centuries of history, the bloodlines of humankind and serpent were mingled. This was an abomination of the highest order, the breeding conducted in secret rituals dedicated to the worship of evil gods.

"The bloodlines grew strong and the *Naga* multiplied and thrived. Under the watchful eye of their Abomination masters, the Halfbloods and the Purebloods spread their coils throughout the lands they infested. They ruled over Japan, and the Han and many other lands.

"It was a dark time of terrible deeds and great darkness moving in the night. Humans were little more than cattle to them. Herds to be worked and culled as necessary. Culled for pleasure, as well as food."

Yoshitsune shivered. "But they were defeated." Knots within the logs popped in the fire. "Their rule was overthrown."

"Yes...the *Tengu* came to these lands. We taught the humans the talent of forging metal and the arts of the sword. The humans stood up to their Naga masters and war began. It was a bitter conflict, with many dark deeds committed by both sides for neither would grant pardon, nor show mercy. A necessary war.

"Eventually, with our aid, one powerful Clan forged an alliance with many others and a bold young hero named Wakamikenu led the war to overthrow Lady Saris."

Yoshitsune gasped.

"Yes," Sojobo nodded, "the very same Saris Taira you now seek to confront. She is old, Yoshitsune. She was old when your first Emperor, Wakamikenu no Mikoto, first took the Chrysanthemum Throne. She is ancient now. Twisted by the relentless passage of centuries with a burning hatred for your kind."

"And ours," Tomiko interrupted.

"Yes, and hatred for ours as well." Sojobo nodded his agreement to her. "She has not forgotten that it was *our* help which allowed the humans to master the military skills necessary to overthrow the *Naga* and drive them into hiding. She will never forgive us for that."

"I will face her."

"You are brave, Yoshitsune, I grant you that. Yet you are also foolish...these are not mere samurai to be challenged and duelled in the streets. Nor are they simple bandits to be hunted down and slain."

"I have slain *Naga*."

"*So ka?*" Sojobo narrowed his eyes. "Purebloods, perhaps."

Yoshitsune made no reply.

"You have slain one or two Purebloods—those who can still pass as ordinary men and women, save for tiny markings."

"The scales on their arms and necks," Tomiko said.

"Yes, some patches of scales. Fangs, more often than teeth. Forked tongues sometimes, though seldom does such breed true. Purebloods can pass for human, but they share the Naga's contempt for humankind." Sojobo paused, firelight playing off his face. "So you have killed one or two...no easy task that but still not a grand challenge. But have you yet faced Halfbloods?"

"Halfbloods? I-I do not know," Yoshitsune admitted. He glanced towards Tomiko, who shrugged in response. "What do they look like?"

"Twisted creatures. Half-man and half-snake. Maybe more than half snake for that matter." Sojobo gently shook his head. "Halfbloods cannot pass as humans—there will be no doubt of their nature. They are most elusive and often remain in hiding, relying on the Purebloods to move amongst humans and carry forth their schemes. When they do appear, it is only for ill. They must not be underestimated. Failing to treat them with due respect will mean your death."

"I am not afraid."

Tomiko shivered. "I am."

Benkei clicked his beak. "And for all the terror that will come from facing a Halfblood, you must still recall the third of the tainted bloodlines."

"The Abominations."

"Yes, young human," Sojobo nodded his head. "No one living now has gazed upon the face of an Abomination. We know not how they look, but I fear there will be nothing of humanity in the face of Lady Saris."

Chapter Twelve

Benkei paused a moment for breath. He warily eyed his opponent, keeping a loose grip on the hilt of his sword. He wore a *haori* and *hakama*, the loose shirt and pants woven from brightly coloured cloth. The dark blue set off the slight iridescent sheen of his feathery green plumage.

Yoshitsune was standing just a few paces away. Sweat covered his bare chest and he was also panting for breath. The human lifted his *shinei* back into position. "Another round?" he inquired as he gave his bamboo sword a quick swing.

"I find myself lacking your youthful stamina," Benkei replied with that cawing laugh of his. "I need a moment longer to recover." He adjusted his grip on his own *shenei*. "Though I do possess something that you yourself lack."

"And what is that?"

"The cunning of age." He threw himself into a sudden attack, slashing at Yoshitsune's head with his sword.

Yoshitsune parried each blow, though he steadily gave ground before Benkei's swift striking attacks.

The clatter of wooden swords striking each other grew louder and louder.

Benkei's blade bounced from his opponent's, and he stumbled.

Yoshitsune pounced on the mistake and brought his blade around in a swing that ended with the tip of the bamboo blade parting the green feathers on Benkei's neck. "I believe that gives this match to me."

The crow-headed *Tengu* nodded and took a step away. "You fight very well," he admitted with some reluctance.

"For a human?"

"Yes...for anyone." Benkei pulled off his *kabuto* helmet and held it loosely in his right hand. "By the Gods, you will rival Sojobo himself before much longer."

Yoshitsune felt his cheeks grow warm and he let his practice blade fall from his fingers. "I doubt that. The *Sensei* is far too skilled for my humble skills to ever equal." He picked up a small cloth from the ground and wiped his face with it.

Benkei set his own practice sword and helmet onto the ground. "So answer me a simple question then," he said softly. "What do you think about Tomiko?"

Yoshitsune turned to face his practice opponent. "What about her?" He seemed confused by the sudden question.

"What are your thoughts about Tomiko?" Benkei glanced around, but the two were alone in the clearing. "Does she excite you, Yoshitsune? Is she a traveling companion...or something more?"

Yoshitsune shook his head. "I don't—"

"Come, you may talk to me freely."

"She has become my friend."

"We figured that much."

"She has proven her valour in battle. She does not shirk from the sight of blood or the eruption of violence." Yoshitsune paused, searching for the right words. "She is a most unusual woman."

Benkei nodded. "She is that," he agreed as he took a drink from a water skin he snatched up from the ground. "She is indeed that." His eyes narrowed. "She is *Tengu* and you are human. Do not forget that."

"How could I?"

Benkei turned away. "Stick to your swordsmanship...there at least you do not embarrass yourself." He walked away leaving Yoshitsune to stare after him.

* * *

"This feels like some child's tale."

Tomiko perched herself delicately atop a fallen log, a faint breeze playing lightly across her face. "Why do you feel that?" she asked. The embroidery on her pale silk kimono was glowing in the sunlight.

"Because of all this." Yoshitsune gestured to their surroundings with both hands. "It is past the height of summer, and yet we stand in a grove of cherry trees that are only just now ready to flower?"

Tomiko looked around the clearing again, seeing it as he would on his first visit. *He sees more than I do,* she thought. *But I have come here so many times in the past. This was always one of my favourite places to come and meditate.*

Yoshitsune was still waiting for an answer.

"We are high on the slopes of Kurama."

"Not that high, Tomiko." He focused his attention on her. "It is as if time flows differently here."

The *Tengu* chuckled softly. "Perhaps it does." Her laughter stilled after a moment.

Yoshitsune stood silent as cicadas chirped at his feet.

Tomiko looked towards her companion. "This particular mountain has long been a refuge for the *Tengu*. We have dwelled here for centuries beyond count." Certainly, it had been for longer than she could remember. "No doubt we have altered the very nature of the valley with our simple presence."

Yoshitsune looked at her more closely. "Do you alter other things?"

"We are creatures of magic," she admitted, "but we cannot alter the course of nature...merely *divert* it slightly." *I cannot* make *you love me,* she thought, *however much I might wish it. I can merely hope that you will someday care for me in that fashion.*

Yoshitsune turned back to his study the horizon beyond the mountain. "I must return to the camp for another practice session."

"Of course." She nodded her head at his words. *Must you leave me so soon? I hardly see you now.* "I am told that you push yourself hard in your training."

"I have much to learn and the teachers here are most instructive."

"You cannot become a master swordsman in a few days."

"I know, Tomiko, but I feel something driving me to learn all that I can."

Tomiko stared at him. *You duel with anyone who will lift his or her sword against you,* she thought. *What drives you so hard? Never have I known anyone like you.* The breeze rustled through the trees, carrying the scent of cherry blossoms to her.

Yoshitsune watched a butterfly flutter past his face. "Do you feel something driving you on, Tomiko?"

"Many things call to me," she replied. "The course of my life is not known to me anymore than it is to you. We *Tengu* have no special foreknowledge of the future. I number no fortune tellers among my kind."

"Nor do I."

Tomiko watched Yoshitsune for a moment. The sunlight played across his face, giving him a youthful glow.

"I feel touched, as if by destiny. The burning of my village was but a catalyst from which some greater fire will be kindled."

"Too many people take all the failures of their lives and bundle them up and call it *destiny,*" Tomiko said bitterly. "Blood once spilled calls for further blood to be shed."

Yoshitsune whirled around to face her. "Would you ask me to ignore my murdered kin?" he asked her. "Would you ask me to abandon our struggle with the *Naga*?"

"No, Lady Saris and her *Naga* must be opposed." She was certain of that. "We both heard the all-but-forgotten history." *Why did Sojobo never speak of such events?* she wondered to herself. *Why did he keep such tales hidden?* Or had she been deemed too young to hear of such horrors?

The gong of a bell tolled out.

"The summons to practice." Yoshitsune took a step away from her. "I must—er, should—go."

"Yes, you should." Tomiko watched the young man hurry away along the path.

"Does your pet Human have any real idea what dangers he faces?"

Tomiko turned her head to stare calmly at Benkei. "You were present at the fires two nights back...you heard all that Sojobo had to say regarding the *Naga*." She turned back towards the sheet of rice paper on the table in front of her. She was kneeling at the low log table, *seiza*-style, and ink brush in hand, though the paper was still pristine.

"Yes, I heard what he told us...and I know some of what he did not."

"He is keeping secrets again?" Tomiko did not sound the least bit surprised by Benkei's revelation. "He always did."

Benkei shifted his position on the log, settling into a more comfortable crouch so that he could watch her paint. He tracked her gaze and saw that she had chosen a spot from which she could overlook the practice field. "Sojobo does only what he thinks is best for the Clan."

"He always did." Her eyes were focused on one particular pair of duellers.

Benkei tilted his head to the left to study her. "Such bitterness in your voice," he chided. "Surely you have felt some stirring of forgiveness for your father."

"He cast me out of the nest!" Tomiko snarled. "He sent me away to wander!" Her fingers gripped the handle of the brush so fiercely that it shattered. She stared at the splinters in dismay.

"You *chose* to wander," Benkei countered with a serenity in his voice that Tomiko could only envy further. "You could have stayed here, among your own kind. Instead, you chose to leave your home nest and flock and travel among the humans for so many years."

"I could not stay here." Tomiko's eyes were drawn back to the practice duel being fought between Yoshitsune and yet another of the *Tengu*.

"He fights well." Benkei chuckled, and then laughed more loudly at her startled expression. "Almost as if he had *Tengu* blood running through his veins."

Tomiko snorted. "Such a thing to say!"

Mori stared down the bridge of his long nose—it was an exceptionally long nose, even for a *Tengu*—and studied the human who knelt before him. "You come before me to seek knowledge."

"*Hai,* Mori-*Sensei.*"

"The art of the blade is not among my skills. I have other talents."

Yoshitsune stared up at the ancient *Tengu*. "So I am told."

Mori nodded once. Most of his feathers had turned grey and he moved about the small hut at a slow shamble. "There are rumours and legends among our Clan," he said slowly, "that the *Naga* have long maintained a stronghold hidden somewhere on the shores of the Chiba river."

"We have heard such rumours ourselves, even before leaving Edo. On our travels, we might a *Kappa*—Kisho, I think his name was—who spoke of such a stronghold with pennants bearing her *mon.*"

"Kisho is surprisingly wise for a humble *Kappa.*" Mori nodded his head slowly. He rubbed the bridge of his enormous nose.

"You know him?"

"I am acquainted with him. As well as any non-*Kappa* might be; *Kappa* are not friendly beings, not even to their own kin." Mori paused for a moment. "It has been many summers saw I last spoke with him. A most violent summer storm caught me alone in the woods and far from shelter. I stumbled into one of his accursed ponds and very nearly drowned."

"He saved you then?"

"After he finished laughing." Mori took a deep breath. "'*It is said that one cannot teach a bird to swim like a fish*,'" he said in a fairly good imitation of Kisho's reedy voice. "'*And now I find that I must thank you for proving it to me.*' Dratted creature."

Yoshitsune smiled. "*Kappa no kawa nagare*," he said. *Even a Kappa might drown.* "I told him that when we met."

Mori chuckled. "Yes," he agreed, "even *Kappas* can drown." His laughter sobered. "Yet we must concern ourselves with the threat of the *Naga*." The elderly *Tengu* leaned back on his heels. "Lady Saris Taira is cunning and has her sight set upon revenge for the ancient defeat of her people. No doubt she has a network of agents lurking within the major cities of Japan, even within Edo and Kyoto too, yet the *Naga* favour lurking in ancient ruins. They need isolation in which to conduct their foul sacrifices."

"Do you know the exact location of these ruins?"

"Of course." Mori slowly blinked his dark eyes. "I was there once...six hundred summers ago I think it was." He turned his gaze towards a rack of pine shelving which groaned under the weight of scrolls and books. "It was very cold that day and I sought shelter...the Purebloods were very reluctant to provide me with a place to sleep. I had to become quite harsh before they would give me even a few coals for my fire."

"You slept beneath their roof?"

"I did."

"I thought they hated you."

"There is enmity between us, but there is also a long-standing truce. We hold no love for one another, true, but neither do we plot to spark another war. The *Naga* operate in the shadows and through deception and secrecy. We *Tengu*...we hold ourselves aloof from the rest of Japan." Mori rubbed at his nose again. "Your own presence not withstanding that is."

* * *

"And so ends another day of practice." Tomiko poured sake into a delicate porcelain cup as Yoshitsune stumbled wearily into the candle-lit hut. *He looks so tired,* she thought. He smelled faintly of flower blossoms too. *He found time to visit the bathhouse,* she thought. *He is such a clean boy.*

"*Domo arigato.*" Yoshitsune drank a deep swallow of the rice wine, and then sank on his knees. "It's not all practice in the field," he told her. "I have lessons in arts other than those of the sword."

Tomiko nodded at his words. "Sojobo always did believe that your mind must be as sharp as your blade." She sat as well, and then gave her kimono a quick tug to adjust the manner in which the folds of cloth rested.

"Sometimes I wonder if I am to become an artist or a warrior."

"You are samurai, are you not?"

"I am..." he paused for a long, awkward, moment, "not truly samurai."

"Because of your lack of noble blood?" Tomiko shrugged. "What does that matter here?" Now it was her turn to pause awkwardly. "Blue blood or not, you will still bleed if you are cut."

"Does that worry you?"

"Should it?" Tomiko attempted to laugh, but her chuckle sounded flat even to her ears. "You fight and grow ever more dangerous. Even the *Naga* will soon learn to fear you."

"I don't need them to fear me. I just need...."

"Yes?" She looked at him as his voice trailed away.

He rose to his feet. "I need some air."

She watched him go.

"The boy has studied hard."

Tomiko did not look up from the table where she was sitting with a piece of rice paper and a brush. "You work him equally hard."

"I did what I must." Sojobo did not sound apologetic. The white-haired *Tengu* closed the door of the hut behind him and his talons clicked against the age-worn pine floorboards. It was a small hut, kept empty for what few visitors came to them, but Tomiko had claimed it for herself and her companion. "One month is far too short a time in which to train a master swordsman. Even for a *Tengu*."

"You claimed that he had talent." Tomiko did not offer to pour sake. She pointedly ignored the small cupboard, which held a meagre selection of refreshments.

"He does have talent. He will make his *sensei* proud."

"If he lives long enough." She tried to mask the bitterness in her voice.

Sojobo gave her a closer look, tilting his head to the left in a bird-like manner. "Tomiko, you are truly worried for his safety."

"He is a young man and they are known to be rash and foolish."

"Whereas you are an old and wise *Tengu*?"

"I am older than his village."

"He does not think about you being old."

Sojobo's word took her by surprise. *He doesn't?* "Does he gossip about me then?" she demanded.

The other *Tengu* clicked his beak in laughter. "He does not speak out of turn."

"He is trapped in affairs above his head."

"He is a brave man." His gaze fell upon a piece of rice paper atop the lacquered cabinet. "Your work?" he asked and she nodded. The drawing was quite obviously of Yoshitsune, standing shirtless with a katana held above his head, ready to strike. "*So ka?*" he mused. "Tomiko, you must know that you cannot love him."

Startled, she looked at the other *Tengu*. "You're still trying to run my life!" she accused. She rose to her feet and advanced across the worn floor towards him. "You never stop!"

Sojobo winced at her tone. "I am merely reminding you of what fate has in store for you both. A human and a *Tengu* cannot be together."

Why not? her heart wailed. "So you say," she said in a cold voice.

"So say I and all of the Elders of *all* the Clans." Sojobo's words were harsh, but there was a note of sympathy in her voice. "This is Law as old as the *Tengu*." He held out his hand. "Tomiko...."

She was silent for a long moment, ignoring his out-stretched hand. "I am supposed to join Mori for tea...if you have said all that you have to say?"

"I have." Sojobo nodded his head to her. "What else can I say to you?"

"Nothing." She opened the door, but paused long to look back at him. "Everything has already been said between us." She let the door swing close.

Chapter Thirteen

Sojobo knelt just inside the small shelter. He lifted his head to stare up at the young man waiting to enter his presence. "Approach." The *Tengu* carried a fan made from seven feathers as a sign of the importance of the ceremony.

Yoshitsune licked his lips with sudden nervousness, and then stepped forward. He wore a *kamishimo*—the ceremonial dress of a samurai. The *kataginu*—the triangle of cloth that covered his shoulders and breast—were dyed a pale blue, to match his skirt-like *hakama*.

"When tea is made with water drawn from the depths of mind, whose bottom is beyond measure, we have what is called cha-no-yu." Sojobo paused and studied his guest. "That was said by a human, you know. Toyotomi Hideyoshi."

"I have not heard of him." Yoshitsune kept his eyes cast downward. The small shelter had walls of rice paper and a peaked roof, thatched with pine branches.

"We shall speak more in time." Sojobo rose to his feet in a single smooth motion. "Wait here until it is time." He offered his guest a deep bow, which Yoshitsune returned, and then backed out of the shelter.

Yoshitsune knelt in the same spot as Sojobo had been when he arrived, and he gazed out at the landscape. The view from that particular spot showed him a waterfall trickling down the mountain and splashing into a shallow pool. The trees of the forest grew close to the water's edge. Birds sang from where they perched on the branches. Yoshitsune focused on his breathing, inhaling and exhaling in a steady manner.

At length, he rose to his feet and stepped back outside.

A bell tolled once.

Yoshitsune stepped away from the shelter. *The time is now,* he thought. He paused next to a small stone basin and dipped his hands into the icy water. He carefully followed the time-honoured ritual to purify himself by washing his hands and rinsing his mouth with the pure water. Then he proceeded to walk through a simple garden along a *roji*—the so-called *dewy path*—to the small rice paper-walled *chaya*.

He removed his *geta* and entered the tea house through a small door. His bare feet felt the roughness of the floorboards. He proceeded first to the *tokonoma* scroll alcove, where he paused to admire the scrolls and other decorations placed therein, before sitting, *seiza*-style, on the tatami. There were several tatami in the main room, as the mats were used in various ways in the tea ceremony. Their simple placement determined how Yoshitsune had walked through the room. When walking on tatami, of course, it was customary to shuffle, thus forcing one to slow down in order to maintain erect posture and to walk quietly, and helped to maintain balance. *It is also a function of wearing kimono,* Yoshitsune reminded himself, *which restricts the length of one's stride. And, of course, one must avoid stepping on the joins between mats; participants must step over such joins when walking in the tea room.*

Sojobo was already kneeling on his own tatami. Without speaking a single word, he offered a careful bow.

Equally silent, Yoshitsune returned it. He sank into *seiza*-posture.

As was proper, Sojobo had waited until his guest arrived before he built the charcoal fire and began heating the water for making the tea.

Yoshitsune waited in respectful silence. *What type of ceremony is this to be?* he wondered. *Will there be a meal, or only the tea?* He had attended other tea ceremonies in the past, and he was eager to see what differences his *Tengu* host might offer. Guests at a ceremony might be served a light, simple *tenshin,* or a special kind of full-course *kaiseki* complete with sake. A meal served now would mean that he would have to return to the waiting shelter until summoned again by his host for the tea itself. *If no meal is going to be served, then Sojobo will proceed directly to the serving of small sweets.* Yoshitsune tried to keep his face serene. *I lack a* kaishi, he thought sadly. Sweets were eaten from special paper called *kaishi*, which each guest carried in a decorative wallet or tucked into the breast of the kimono.

Sojobo proceeded to ritually clean each of his utensiles, following the ritual by doing so in the presence of his guest and in a precise order and using prescribed motions. Each utensil—including the tea bowl, the whisk, and the tea scoop—was then precisely placed in a particular arrangement on their tatami.

Yoshitsune watched with due attentiveness. In deference to tradition, conversation was kept to a minimum throughout the tea ceremony, and he felt no need to speak. He simply relaxed and enjoyed the atmosphere created by the sounds of the water and fire, the smell of the subtle incense and tea, and the beauty and simplicity of the tea house and its seasonally appropriate decorations.

When the ritual cleaning and preparation of the utensils was complete, Sojobo placed a carefully measured amount of green tea powder into the bowl, added the appropriate amount of hot water, and then whisked the tea using set movements. When the tea was ready, Sojobo poured it out into a small porcelain bowl.

Yoshitsune watched closely.

Sojobo bowed to Yoshitsune.

Yoshitsune raised the laquered bowl in a gesture of respect to his host. He then rotated the bowl to avoid drinking from its front and took a sip. "It is most excellent," he murmured, before taking two more sips. He then wiped the rim, rotating the bowl back to its original position, and returned it to Sojobo with another bow.

The elderly *Tengu* smiled, but remained silent.

Yoshitsune allowed the serenity of the *chaya* to fill him. *I have partaken in tea ceremonies before,* he thought. *I know the correct traditional responses, though I am not trained to actually conduct such a ceremony.* He could tell that Sojobo was impressed with his manners.

Sojobo handed the tea bowl back to him and Yoshitsune drank again. He returned the empty to bowl to his *sensei* with another bow.

Sojobo then proceeded to clean the utensils in preparation for putting them away.

"May this unworthy student see the utensiles?" Yoshitsune made the ritual request in a low tone.

"You may." Sojobo nodded. He nodded with satisfaction as Yoshitsune examined and admired each utensil, including the tea caddy and the tea scoop.

Yoshitsune was careful in how he held each of the precious items, using a piece of brocaded cloth for that purpose. Every single thing had to be treated with extreme care and reverence as he had no doubt that the pieces were priceless. *Each of them is likely an irreplaceable antique,* he thought. "Handcrafted by yourself?" he asked aloud.

"By my grandfather long before we came to these islands."

The age of the delicate porcelain in his hands almost made Yoshitsune fear that might drop the bowl. "These are treasures without price," he said.

"What good is treasure if it cannot be enjoyed?" Sojobo countered.

"What good indeed?"

Sojobo collected his utensils and returned them to their place on the mat.

And thus the bon temae *ceremony ends.* Yoshitsune rose to his feet and slowly and carefully crossed the tatami to the door. He paused, turned, and bowed respectfully back to Sojobo.

The *Tengu* followed him to the door. He bowed and then gestured for Yoshitsune to step outside.

Yoshitsune froze in his steps.

During the hours-long ceremony, the garden had filled with *Tengu.*

When did they come to be here? he wondered in shock. *They were so quiet while they have been waiting. What can this mean?* He fumbled the *geta* back on his feet.

Sojobo stepped through the door of the *chaya* and stopped beside him. "We are not yet done with ceremony, my young apprentice."

"*So ka, Sensei?*" Yoshitsune hastily dropped onto his knees. He caught a glimpse of Tomiko standing next to Benkei in the crowd. They were both wearing fine kimonos.

"No, there is still something to be done." Sojobo clicked his beak.

Mori shuffled forward, dressed in a richly patterned kimono. He was a carrying a *saya*, the lacquered stand holding two sheathed swords.

Yoshitsune stared, his eyes wide, until they began to burn and he was finally forced to blink. *It cannot be!*

"I present you with these blades, forged by skilled artisans many centuries ago." The long katana caught the sunlight and sparkled as Sojobo drew it from its artfully decorated *saya*. "This katana was wielded by your first Emperor, when he overthrew the *Naga* and established his rule over the Home Islands." He set the katana onto a small piece of linen cloth that another *Tengu* had hastily laid out.

The *Tengu* child stared at Yoshitsune with wide brown eyes as he backed away.

"This is the matching honour blade." Sojobo set the *wakizashi* down onto the linen cloth so that the short sword matched the katana.

Yoshitsune stared down at the carved ivory hilts and razor-edged blades, then hastily lowered his head even more. "I am unworthy to bare such blades."

"Nonsense!" Tomiko burst out. "You have proven your worth many times over."

Sojobo glanced towards her.

Tomiko stared back at him. "You have mastered your lessons—no one here would gainsay that." Certainly none of the other *Tengu* seemed eager to speak up. "It seems appropriate that you should gain possession of these blades."

Sojobo nodded his head. "Tomiko is correct. Outspoken," he added, "and once again showing her usual lack of respect for tradition and ceremony."

Tomiko closed her mouth and hastily returned to her place at Benkei's side.

That crow-headed *Tengu* was clicked his beak softly in laughter.

"Tomiko has told us of your bravery in battle against the *Naga* many times," Sojobo continued. "We have watched you train, pushing yourself as hard as your teachers could push you. You carry a warrior's soul, Minamoto no Yoshitsune, and you are worthy to wear these blades, just as Wakamikenu no Mikoto proved himself."

Yoshitsune bowed deeply to his *sensei*. "I hear your words, *Sensei*, and I cannot argue with you." He paused a moment. "I have no choice but to accept this princely gift." He reached out with his hand and, after a final moment of hesitation, picked up the katana and stared at it anew. "The swords of the first Emperor himself," he whispered. "Legend says that these blades were lost centuries ago." His narrow face bore a puzzled frown. "But how did you come to possess these blades?"

"I helped to forge them." Sojobo shrugged as Yoshitsune's eyes widened.

"There is a sour taste to the wind." Sojobo offered that comment as he drew his *kimono* more tightly around his torso. He was walking through the village with Tomiko at his side and Yoshitsune trailing after.

Yoshitsune kept staring at his new swords, as if unable to believe that they were actually his own possessions.

Young *Tengu* darted past, playing some childish game.

Tomiko watched them running past with a smile. The sword-gifting ceremony had broken up and the village's inhabitants had returned to their usual pastimes.

"Do you feel a storm coming?" Yoshitsune looked up at the sky, but it was clear and blue. He saw no clouds on this side of the mountain.

Sojobo shook his head. "Not a thunderstorm, but something...."

Tomiko drew her own cloak more tightly around her body as they left Yoshitsune many paces behind. "You sense danger?" she asked quietly.

"These are dangerous times for us all. They grow ever more so." Sojobo looked at her. "You two should make preparations to depart."

Tomiko nodded, but her tone was reluctant. "I would not wish to remain in any nest where I am not welcome."

Sojobo looked at her, his mouth half-open.

"Are we in danger?" Yoshitsune asked as he approached the two *Tengu*. He rested his hands on the hilts of his swords, ready to draw them in an instant. His eyes rested on Tomiko and a smile played across his lips.

"Not precisely." Tomiko sighed. *He looks so deadly,* she thought. *He carries himself like a warrior.*

Chapter Fourteen

Standing in the clearing, the two embraced. Blossoms from the cherry trees fell around them like sweet-scented snow.

"*O-medeto*," Tomiko whispered to him. "Congratulations."

"I never expected to accepted like this." Yoshitsune rested his hand on the hilt of his katana for a moment, and then put his arms back around her. "To be trained by *Tengu* and then to be granted such blades to carry...it is overwhelming!"

"The training merely brought out your natural talents," Tomiko replied. "You already had training when we first met."

"Rough and unwonted," he protested. "Only the most worthy and blessed swordsmen can claim the benefits of such training and of such teachers. I can only think of twenty such heroes in history."

He looks so youthful when he smiles, Tomiko thought.

"I need you, Tomiko."

"I feel the same way, Yoshitsune." There were blossoms in her hair now, as they reluctantly broke apart. She stared up at his face, searching his expression carefully.

"Please, say that you will never leave me."

Tomiko heard the words and felt her heard race. "I will stay with you as long as I can, but the dangers—"

"I will protect you."

Tomiko stared at him sadly. "We cannot truly be together...I am *Tengu* and you are human." Abruptly, she embraced him...and felt the hilt of his new sword dig into her belly. "Nonetheless, I will stay at your side for as long as I can," she promised.

He stared into her tear-filled eyes. "Tomiko, I think that I—"

"Hush." She pressed her finger against his lips. "Do not say it." Tears filled her eyes. "Do not speak that word. Just enjoy the moment."

The blossoms continued to fall around them.

Yoshitsune carefully retied his *obi* around his waist. "We should start walking back to Edo," he declared. "I fear what evils the Cult might be getting up too in our absence. We have been gone too long."

"The time was necessary." Tomiko gestured towards him with her hand. "You needed time and training to master the arts of the sword. And you needed to earn those fine new blades."

"You speak the truth," he agreed. "These swords are truly prizes suitable only for one both skilled enough and worthy to wield them." He licked his lips. "But I must wonder if I am truly worthy?"

"You have the blades...then you will prove yourself worthy." Tomiko paused. *Or get yourself killed while trying to prove such worth.* The swords were no simple gift. *Sojobo was never known for his subtlety.*

"Nonetheless, we have lingered here long enough. We must return to Edo."

"Tomorrow." Tomiko rose gracefully to her feet and brushed leaves and cherry blossoms from her hair and from her lilac kimono. "Tomorrow will be soon enough."

"We will need provisions."

"Do not concern yourself, Yoshitsune. We will have all that we need to travel. My people are generous and will aid us as they can." She gestured calmly towards the towering mountain. "The pathway is just ahead."

They walked back towards the camp at a steady pace. The breeze had died away and the forest was still.

Tomiko glanced at her companion.

Yoshitsune was walking with a smile on his face. "The past month has flown by far more quickly than I would have dreamed. This place truly is magical."

"Sometimes time flies past so quickly that is it gone before you have a chance to catch hold. Time is too often wasted."

"No time spent with you is ever wasted."

Tomiko smiled at his words.

Finally, only a thin screen of pine trees separated them from the clearing.

"We want the human man-child," a voiced hissed from just beyond the pines and they both froze.

"He is not here." Sojobo's voice was firm and resolute as he answered. It carried clearly to the listeners.

"He was here, old one. You are hiding him."

"We hide no one."

"*Naga*," Yoshitsune whispered. He gripped the hilt of his new katana and carefully drew it from its sheath.

Tomiko hastily gripped his shoulder. *Don't do anything rash!* she pleaded silently.

"There is no mistaking that hissing accent of theirs," he added.

"I know. We heard it often enough in the streets of Edo." Tomiko reached out to carefully push aside a branch so that she could stare through the thin screen of pines.

A dozen men and women stood on the pathway, most holding short bows. Half of them wore cloaks; the others were in simple clothing. They could almost be mistaken for ordinary slim-hipped humans, save for their unblinking eyes and patches of scales on their arms and necks.

One woman, with a particularly flat face, gestured with her left hand. "Do not seek to interfere in our affairs, Sojobo," she warned. Her black hair was drawn into a tight braid that hung down her back to well below her knees. "Matters may not proceed as you expect."

Sojobo stared back at her, his own expression one of impassive calm. "The *Tengu* do as they please. We have told you that before, Kalbra, when you were last here. We are neither the servants nor the slaves of your Lady Saris. *We* did not lose the ancient war."

The woman hissed, baring her fangs. She hastily regained her composure. "My Mistress can be generous to her friends...and she has an equally generous fate for those who style themselves as her enemies."

"Get off my mountain."

Kalbra nodded her head sadly. "As you wish, Sojobo. This will be on your talons." She raised both of her hands. "Kill everyone here."

The *Naga* threw aside their cloaks. Those who did not carry bows now drew their curved scimitars. Several of the males had colourfully stripped scales—the patterns and colouration of poisonous snakes—across their bare torsos.

Sojobo drew his own *katana*. "You do not wish to do this, Kalbra."

"He buys time for us," Tomiko whispered even as the *Naga's* hissing laughter came to them. "Run, Yoshitsune!" She tugged at his shoulder, but he refused to move. She shook her head regretfully, but turned to watch, as he did, as the master swordsman fought.

Arrows sped from four of the bows and with the barest flicks of his wrist, the *Tengu* swatted the arrows from the air with his *katana*.

"He is amazing," Yoshitsune whispered.

Sojobo whirled on his feet and sliced his blade through the chest of one of his scimitar-wielding foes who fell with a hissed cry.

Kalbra watched with her lips bared in a snarl.

Sojobo crossed blades with another *Naga*, and kicked the man aside.

One of the more snake-like *Naga* slipped in close, then hissed and then spat foul venom from his mouth.

The elderly *Tengu* stumbled and fell to the ground, gasping.

"No!" Yoshitsune charged through the pine branches and his slashing blade cut through the *Naga's* neck.

"Father!" Tomiko threw herself at another of the *Naga*. Her *bo* struck the creature in his chest and cracked ribs.

"It's the boy!" Kalbra hissed. She drew a curved dagger from her green *obi*. "He must die!"

The *Naga* charged.

"No more deaths!" Benkei flung himself from the treetops. His katana sliced the hands from a bowman before the *Naga* even registered his arrival.

Kalbra slashed at Yoshitsune.

He blocked the dagger blow with his sword.

Tomiko cracked her *bo* against the skull of another assailant.

A slashing scimitar tore the silk sleeve of Benkei's kimono. "Damn you!" He slashed back.

Tomiko fell to her knees on the ground beside Sojobo. "He's still breathing!"

"Summon aid!" Yoshitsune called as he struck down another of Sojobo's would-be assassins. "I can hold them."

Benkei cawed loudly. "Assassins!" he screamed at the top of his lungs. "Defend yourselves!" His katana clanged against a *Naga's* scimitar. "Assassins!"

The creature hissed at him.

Kalbra slashed her dagger past Yoshitsune's face.

He dodged away from her.

Tomiko bent low over her father.

An arrow flashed past Yoshitsune's head.

Benkei killed one *Naga* and then immediately engaged another.

A bell gonged in the distance.

Yoshitsune stepped away from Kalbra, and then abruptly he turned and dashed in close. His katana caught her chest and sliced through her ribs.

The dagger dropped from her lifeless fingers to hit the ground with a dull thud.

* * *

A skeletal cobra of incomprehensible proportions loomed above the towers and buildings of Edo Castle, its elongated skull brushing against the pale moon. Smoke from scores of fires raging throughout the city rose to coil slowly about its face. Its jaws gaped open, revealing katana-like fangs, and then a forked tongue lashed out, shattering buildings. It seemed to laugh as the screams of dying men and women rang out in some unholy dirge.

* * *

The clearing was quiet and sombre beneath the pendulous clouds that wreathed the peak of Mount Kamura.

Tengu moved amongst their huts and to and from the caves in a furtive manner unlike their usual boisterous natures. Small groups gathered and muttered softly to one another before continuing towards their various destinations. Many cast nervous looks over their shoulders, their eyes watching the forest. The handful of fledglings that were outside of their homes, played quietly under the watchful eyes of several armed *Tengu*.

Tomiko stood near a smoking fire pit, a feathered cloak drawn tightly around her. Memories of the previous night's nightmare still haunted her, ghostly images of the skeletal cobra still dancing before her dark eyes.

Yoshitsune approached her with slow steps, hesitant to bother her yet drawn to provide what comfort he could. He wore his own simple *hakama* and *haori*, his new swords held by his red *obi*. "Is he going to be all right?" he asked in a soft voice.

"The healers are with him right now." Tomiko kept her own voice under tight control and the strain was plainly evident. "Healers have been with him all night. The *Naga* poison is particularly virulent."

"I'm sorry."

Tomiko stared at the embers.

"I owe much to Sojobo-san," Yoshitsune said. "He has taught me far more than I would have dreamed possible in the short time we have been here. And yesterday he fought and risked all of you rather than betray me."

"You were welcomed here under our protection. Sojobo could not give you up to the *Naga*...even if we trusted them."

Yoshitsune cautiously placed his right hand on her shoulder. "The *Naga* would—"

"The *Naga* would have killed all of us. If they had come by night, to have struck while we slept, none of us would have survived."

"But they came by daylight."

"They wanted you." *And why?* Tomiko wondered. *What makes you so special that they would single you out so fiercely?*

"I brought this upon you." There was no mistaking the bitterness in his voice.

"You did not," she told him honestly. "They hate my people." Tomiko took a deep breath. "We do not hate them, you know. We do not fear them, however much they might wish that we do. We *know* them. We remember that long-past war."

"Which your people won."

"In aid of your own, Yoshitsune."

The young man's eyes were staring towards the cave where the old *Tengu* was being tended. "And now Sojobo pays the price."

Tomiko stared glumly into the ashes. "It has been whispered that Sojobo possesses the strength of a thousand ordinary *Tengu*. We shall learn the truth of that." She stood rigidly, as if her back had turned to ice.

The young human shook his head grimly. "If I hadn't come here, then the *Naga* would never have come here." His gaze moved and rested on the still smouldering remains of a burned-out hut. "They came at us in such great numbers." He removed his hand from her shoulder and rested it on the hilt of his katana. "Mori told me that there were at least three troupes involved in this attack. Nearly sixty *Naga*." *None of whom lived through the night.*

"It's not your fault," Tomiko told him in a dull voice. She still had not turned to look at him. "I brought you here. You needed the training."

"We have stayed here too long." Yoshitsune blinked wearily. "Assassins dog our every footstep." The cherry trees were nearly barren now, their bare branches twisting in the cold wind like skeletal fingers. He frowned, but Tomiko didn't seem to notice anything amiss about the clearing.

Benkei emerged from the cave, his slow tread proclaiming his great weariness. He still wore his ripped kimono, with dried blood staining its sleeves. Most of the stains were the greenish blood of the *Naga*.

"How is Sojobo?" Yoshitsune demanded of him.

Tomiko whirled around. "Is my father—?"

"He sleeps."

Tomiko's rigid posture slumped.

Yoshitsune closed his eyes for a moment and his lips moved in a silent prayer.

"Will he recover?"

Benkei shrugged. "Ah, Tomiko, who can know another's fate?" he asked sombrely. "If the Gods wish him to join Them, then he will likely not last another night."

With a crack of thunder, white snowflakes began to fall.

The smoke from eight funeral pyres was strong in the air. The clearing was filled with *Tengu,* clad in white *kimonos* and cloaks.

"Rise to the Heavens and soar forever more!" Mori croaked as the cold wind tugged at his feathered cloak. "Fly free amid the clouds."

Yoshitsune wore his full samurai finery, with his swords at his waist. He looked out of place amid the bird-like *Tengu,* but they had welcomed him among them.

The assembled *Tengu* cawed softly and then lifted their voices in a mournful dirge.

Tomiko stood near one pyre. Her dark eyes were shadowed. "Eight of us died here," she told Yoshitsune.

"And so did nearly sixty of our foes."

She shook her head slowly. "That is far too many of us for one time. Our lives are usually so long...for them to be cut short by violence is disturbing."

"It is the way of the world. The strong shape the course of history. The weaker must bow, or perish. Yet the strong must also follow the path of honour and not strive to take advantage of the weak."

Tomiko looked at him.

Mori hobbled towards them on his twisted feet. "One cannot argue with fate," he agreed in a tired voice.

"No, one cannot."

Mori clutched his cloak more tightly about himself. "You speak of honour, young samurai?"

"Yes, I did. I was saying that the strong must fulfill the demands of honour. The stronger one is, the more important honour becomes."

"A profound statement. Good words to live by." Mori nodded his head, his dark eyes narrowing as he studied Yoshitsune more closely. "The *Naga* are strong. They were stronger once, long ago."

"They acted without honour. It cost them their empire."

"Indeed...but they seek to regain it." His gaze flicked towards the still-blazing fires. "Their ambition will demand a high price."

"We've paid enough!" Tomiko protested.

Mori turned to stare at her. He tapped the end of his enormous nose. "Have we now?"

Tomiko stared back.

Yoshitsune paced towards one of the pyres. All of the gathered *Tengu* were watching him. "Eight of you have given their lives defending their families and nests." He drew his katana. "You shall be avenged," he vowed.

Chapter Fifteen

The mist was cool and the sky overcast.

"A miserable day for traveling." Yoshitsune trudged slowly on, his feet sinking into the mud with every step. The sudden snow had turned to rain, further down the mountainside, which had then poured for five days. Even after the rains stopped, the air was still damp and the sky still dark with clouds. He had obtained a warm cloak from the *Tengu* before leaving, and he kept it pulled close to cut the wind.

"We could not linger. Our time is far too precious to be wasted." Tomiko plodded along the path at a steady pace. Mount Kumara had fallen far behind them and now was lost to sight. "We have wasted too much time already."

"Tomiko, the last few days were not wasted." He paused, as if uncertain of how to continue. "We could have stayed there longer. Your father needs you at his side."

"I can do nothing for him." Tomiko shook her head. "He sleeps for now. He has slept since the attack." *A magical trance that I hope will do him good.* "The healers believe that he will recover." She tried to sound hopeful but she could not convince herself of that belief.

"You could have stayed at his side. I can continue this quest without you."

"I have never been a very dutiful daughter," Tomiko admitted, a trace of her old personality coming to the front. "Our relationship has been...strained of late. I *could* have remained there...but you need me more." She stopped, and turned around to face him.

He took a step towards her. "I do need you," he admitted softly.

"Then I could not stay at my father's side."

Yoshitsune shook his head. "Tomiko, a few more days would have made no great difference in our quest. Our journey back to Edo will require weeks unless we find horses. I fear that the *Naga* will set their plans into motion long before we arrive."

"Then we shall find ourselves horses." Tomiko nodded with a sudden decisiveness. "There is a rice merchant living near the village of Hikone who owes me a favour. I intend to collect."

Yoshitsune stared at her in surprise. "Just like that?"

"*Hai*! Just like that." Tomiko gazed up the highway. "Ah!" She hurried forward, her bare feet certain of their footing, and then paused a moment to study a roadside marker. "Come, we should be able to reach Hikone by late afternoon."

Yoshitsune read the marker as he hurried past it to catch up with her. "Late afternoon?" he asked after making the calculations.

"Yes, by tomorrow's sun." Tomiko's broke into a smile. "Assuming that the sun does break through these clouds."

* * *

Tomiko paced along the hard-packed dirt at a steady pace. The road, which had wound through the forest, had been all but deserted. *We have only seen a handful of peddlers and one patrol of samurai. We might as well be back in the mountains as traveling along one of the Shogun's highways.*

"Do you think we are near the Chiba yet?"

Tomiko frowned at Yoshitsune's question, and then shook her head. "We should be getting very close though." She looked up at the sky, trying to gauge the position of the late afternoon sun. "We'll end up near Tsuchiura at this rate. I don't know anyone around there."

"We owe Hosokawa Hiroshi thanks for giving us that ride."

"I told you that he owed me a favour."

"That you did."

"Still we were blessed by fortune that we arrived just as he was sending wagons to the Shogun's estates north of Edo." The opportunity to ride in the wagons along the highways had saved them considerable time. *And no doubt, the presence of Hiroshi's guards saved us from further ambushes by the* Naga. Surely, their journey was not going by unnoticed by their enemies. *His debt to me is truly repaid.* "Fortune smiles on us."

"I pray that the Gods continue to favour us."

"Second thoughts, Yoshitsune?"

The young samurai shook his head. "I am bound by both my oath and by my honour to see this through. I am merely...concerned with your presence."

After all this time? she thought. "Don't be."

"We are set on a course to strike at the heart of our enemies...this is not a safe place for either of us."

"I will not turn back. The *Naga* attacked my home and killed my friends—as they did yours. I wish to return the favour." *A fairly bold move on our part,* she thought. *Scouting enemy territory alone. Perhaps we will catch the* Naga *off-guard. Perhaps we can find some solution to thwart the schemes of this Lady Saris.* Her lips twitched into a smile. *Or else we will simply have found a truly novel method of* seppuku.

Yoshitsune paused near a gnarled pine and shook a stone from inside his sandal. "This is a dangerous place. The cult's fortress should be along here somewhere."

"If Mori was recalling things right."

"Don't you trust him?"

Tomiko considered her words before voicing her reply. "He is old...ancient even by *Tengu* standards. It is possible that he was mistaken in his memories. Time and distance all too often become fluid things to the elderly."

"He seemed so certain when he spoke." Yoshitsune rested his hand on the hilt of his sheathed katana.

"We *are* getting close to the Chiba...we will soon learn if he was mistaken."

"I hope not. I would hate to see this journey of ours wasted. We have so little time available to us if we hope to stop their schemes from becoming reality."

"If we cannot find their lair, then what do you propose?"

"We might venture back to Edo."

"I hear hesitation in your words."

Yoshitsune nodded. "I do not feel that returning to the capitol is the right decision for us," he admitted. He continued to study the forest, his eyes darting from bush to tree as if he expected to be ambushed at any moment. "Tomiko, I greatly value your guidance and wisdom."

"I am not certain what to advise."

"Perhaps we should have sought other companions then. Some of your kin—"

"The others would not leave the mountains." Tomiko shook her grey-haired head with grim certainty. "They are *unwilling* to involve themselves in the affairs of humans."

"Yet we are dealing with *Naga*."

"And they attacked our nests...the Flock will seek to protect itself first and foremost. They will stand ready to defend the nests, but I do not know if they will openly battle the *Naga* on other battlefields. The ancient war was long ago." Very long ago. "Sojobo might have decided to oppose Saris and under his leadership the others would march, but now he lays in a healing trance."

Yoshitsune licked his lips. "If Sojobo...fails to waken, who will lead the Flock?"

"I do not know." Tomiko was frowning again. She continued walking, focusing at the road under her feet.

"You're his daughter."

"We do not pass leadership of the Flock through hereditary blood. The rites of succession are more...complicated. It is not easily explained to a Human."

"I understand."

Tomiko's broke into a smile. "I do not understand all the rites myself."

Yoshitsune chuckled. "Human affairs are confusing and oftentimes needlessly complicated as well. Why should those of the *Tengu* be any different?"

"Why indeed?" Tomiko laughed.

Yoshitsune's smile grew broader. *It has been too long since she laughed aloud like that.* He had missed the sound.

The trees parted and a stretch of the slow-flowing Chiba River was revealed to them.

"It seems that Mori was not entirely forgetful," Tomiko admitted as she stared at the stone ruins that loomed near the water's edge. The last of her laughter grew silent.

Yoshitsune's grip tightened on his katana. The ruined temple exuded an aura of darkness. "We have found the lair of Saris and her *Naga*."

Tomiko nodded. "Yes, we have…and now we must be cautious."

The temple was long-abandoned, or so it appeared.

"Most of the buildings are little more than crumbling shells." Yoshitsune shook his head as he studied them from where they crouched among the trees. "Open to the sky and to the rain alike."

"That part seems intact." Tomiko gestured to one of the central buildings that seemed to be in good repair. "Not even the *Naga* would enjoy living in the bitter weather."

"Are you sure of that?"

"No." A banner bearing the *mon* of Lady Saris flapped in the stiff wind. "That is her sign."

"Yes." Yoshitsune shook his head. "But the *mon* alone is not proof that this is the lair of the *Naga*. Saris might have stolen some noble *mon* to further hide her own identity."

Tomiko gave her companion a surprised look. *A most intelligent thought,* she mused as she reappraised how she thought of him. "I never thought of that," she admitted aloud and he smiled. "Come, we shall move closer and seek firm proof."

"Be careful."

"Always." Tomiko led him through a copse of trees towards the river's shoreline.

Yoshitsune frowned as they crept through the waist-tall grass. "We seemed to find the ruins fairly easily."

"Suspiciously so?"

"Yes. We looked long and hard in Edo and found little beyond rumour. We wander the countryside and hear even less rumours, save from *Kappa* and *Tengu*. And now, as we venture along the highway, we find this place."

"We were told where the *Naga* laired. The Shogun's samurai lack such willing informants as we came across." Tomiko wondered if the samurai would have listened to *Kappa* or *Tengu*. She stopped near the river's edge. "Caverns," she gestured further up the shoreline at dark openings in the rocks. "I see only one dock...with no boats tied to it."

"We were told that Saris has a fleet of barges."

"They must be kept inside, out of casual sight." Tomiko paused and studied the lone dock again. *Or else they have already left this place*, she thought grimly. *Could we have arrived here too late?*

Yoshitsune was studying the dock through narrowed eyes. "Saris obviously values her privacy."

"Apparently."

Yoshitsune rested his hand on his sheathed katana. "Tomiko, perhaps you should wait here."

"And allow *you* to wander blindly into danger?" she asked.

"I'm just going to take a look around. I won't start any fights."

"Those temple ruins are supposedly the lair of the *Naga*. This is a very dangerous place for either of us to be." She kept her voice calm. "It is the heart of our enemy's stronghold. This is their greatest fortress."

"Maybe. We must find out if the *Naga* are really here. The Lady Saris who flies that *mon* might not be the Lady Saris we are expecting."

Tomiko gave him another appraising look. "Is there any doubt?"

"Not in my mind, but the Shogun will not see things as we do. If we are to return here with an army to clean out this den of vipers, then we must have proof that no man may doubt."

"A good thought," she admitted, surprised that he had thought of it. "But we will go among there together. If these ruins are indeed the lair of the foul creatures we hunt, then we might take them off guard by appearing together."

"It might be a trap."

Oh, it's almost certainly a trap...but is it one set for us? "It's just a temple, right?" Tomiko pulled her *geta* from within her pack and began to cram her feet into them. *And with but a minimum of cursing the foul things!* she thought, feeling her toes get pinched. "We are merely two humble pilgrims seeking shelter for the night." She smiled at him. "Coming?"

He smiled at her. "You are a most amazing woman."

She offered him a bow. "I am full of surprises."

The main building was empty. The two had ventured through an open door and into a central courtyard. Many doorways stood open, revealing the empty rooms beyond them. Others possessed doors, currently closed against the elements.

Tomiko looked around, carefully studying the appearance of the temple.

"A very basic kitchen." Yoshitsune made that announcement after he had passed cautiously beyond one doorway. He looked into another alcove. "Not much in the pantry. Just bushels of rice and sacks of dried vegetables."

"The very model of a temple inhabited by pious men."

"Who are all mysteriously absent."

Tomiko nodded and turned to push open another door and gazed into what was apparently a dormitory. *None of the doors are locked or barred...the inhabitants apparently have nothing to hide.* "Perhaps they are out in the fields or on other labours." There was considerable work required to keep a temple operating and habitable. *They could be simple monks working in nearby fields.*

"We saw no fields as we approached. The forest presses close upon us."

"The land may not be suitable for farming. The fields could be just beyond that copse." She gestured towards one stand of pines.

Yoshitsune shook his head as he followed her into the dormitory. "Why not believe the supposed monks are currently engaged in prayer?"

"Or else they have ventured into the mountains and been slain." Tomiko kicked at one futon. "It stinks in here." She rubbed at her enormous nose. "It smells of old dried snakeskin."

"I smell nothing."

"Well, you are only human."

Yoshitsune pushed at another door. He frowned when it did not open easily. He pushed again. "This one is locked."

"Why would an inner door be locked and not the outer one?"

"I have no idea." Yoshitsune pushed at the door a third time. "Ah, it's not truly locked...merely stuck." He applied more pressure and the door slowly opened with a squeal from its hinges.

Tomiko winced at the noise, but the temple was apparently truly deserted.

"What is this?" Yoshitsune stepped through and Tomiko hurried after him.

The doorway opened into a small room. The floor dropped rapidly away, becoming a ramp descending into the depths of the earth.

"Do we follow it?"

"It is too late to turn back now." Yoshitsune rested his hand on the hilt of his katana, though he did not yet draw it. "We must follow this road to its end."

"Indeed, we have little choice." Tomiko gestured. She had gripped her small *tanto*, but did not draw the dagger from her *obi*. "Follow me."

"No, you follow me." He pushed ahead of her.

Tomiko snorted. "*Youth*!"

The ramp curved downwards as they walked on for what seemed like hours but surely could not have been. Pillars were spaced even along the roughly tunnelled walls, holding thick beams to support the ceiling, and far-spaced lanterns gave a ghostly blue light as they burned.

Yoshitsune eyed several of the lanterns in curiosity as they passed them by, then he finally approached one. "Beetles!" he exclaimed as he peered inside the coarse paper.

Tomiko took a look for herself. "Yes, they are beetles," she agreed, before continuing to walk. *I won't tell him that those lanterns are actually wasp nests,* she thought. *I do not wish to alarm him. I just hope we do not encounter any of those wasps.* She couldn't hear any buzzing, so it must be safe.

"They glow like fireflies." Yoshitsune was still staring at the beetles.

Tomiko glanced back at him. "Did you expect the *Naga* to use torches?"

"Well, yes." Yoshitsune smiled sheepishly as he hurried after her. "I guess that I did not expect them to be so different."

"They are ancient creatures. There are stranger things in the world than glowing beetles." Tomiko smiled at his embarrassed expression. "Sometimes I forget just how young you truly are."

Yoshitsune snorted. "It's damp down here."

"Snakes like the dampness." Tomiko watched water slowly drip from the ceiling to splash onto the hard-packed ground. "I do not care for such places."

"We could turn back."

"No, we have come this far. We will continue."

They walked on, their soft footsteps echoed from the ceiling.

How far down are we going? *Tomiko wondered. Are we going to venture to the very gates of Yomi itself? No doubt, Saris and her Naga would be comfortable dwelling in the Land of Filth. She glanced towards her companion.*

Yoshitsune was walked forward with a resolved expression on his face.

The ramp curved more sharply and they rounded that turn together. The tunnel opened abruptly into a small cavern with an archway built into the far wall. A curtain hung across it, blocking the contents from view.

A kimono-clad woman was standing near the archway, and now she slowly turned towards them. "*Konichi-wa*," she said politely, with a peculiar accent. She did not appear to be surprised by their appearance. Her pale eyes flicked across them both with a measuring stare.

"*Konichi-wa*," Tomiko said with a shallow bow.

Yoshitsune eyed the woman carefully. She appeared beautiful, slender hipped, with waist-length black hair. Her eyes were unblinking as she stared at them. Exceptionally long nails tipped both her fingers and her bare toes.

Her dark eyes narrowed and Yoshitsune hastily offered his own polite bow, and then took a step further away from her.

"Your pardon. We have come to the temple to seek shelter for the night," Tomiko said with another small bow. "We saw the ruins, but did not think anyone still dwelled here. My grandson found this ramp and we followed the trail of lanterns down here." She paused, attempting to appear simple and bewildered. "After all, lighted lanterns must have *someone* to tend them. I hope that we have not trespassed."

"The Temple is open to all," the woman said in her peculiar silibrant accent. "Please, enter and make yourself comfortable."

"Thank you. I am Uzume. This is my grandson," she repeated.

"I am named Lyrous." She brushed her hands along her blue-green kimono to straighten it. "Please, follow me and I will introduce you to our esteemed Elder. Through here." She led them through the curtain and into another tunnel.

"I have heard," Yoshitsune said as they walked along yet another curving ramp lit by more lanterns, "that this land is owned by a Lady Saris."

Lyrous nodded. "It is."

"Would it be permissible to seek an audience with her?"

"Why?"

"I am a samurai, currently *ronin*." He lowered his head, as if shamed by the admission.

"I am not certain Lady Saris would have any use for a masterless samurai." Her lips twitched in a half-smile. "You may ask her, of course." She gestured to a curtain-blocked archway. "Through there, please."

Chapter Sixteen

The archway opened into a torch-lit cavern. Thick columns, each one carved into the likeness of a hooded cobra, lined the walls and held up the roof.

Yoshitsune eyed them with some dismay.

Tomiko gazed about herself with wide eyes.

Lush curtains and tapestries were strung between the columns, covering the walls or hiding other alcoves. Rich incense filled the air with a spicy scent.

"Lady Saris?" Lyrous called out.

One of the curtains rustled. "Yes?" The speaker had the same accent as their guide, though her deep voice was even more silibrant.

"You have visitors seeking an audience with your august presence."

A curtain shifted and Saris emerged.

Yoshitsune gasped.

Tomiko blinked repeatedly.

Saris was beautiful and her flat face had an exotic otherness to it. Her hair was lank, a paler hue of jade than her egg-shaped eyes. Her alien beauty ended there, however, for her body was that of a snake, with reticulated emerald-green patterns running along the thirty-foot length of her scaly body.

Lyrous bowed deeply to her mistress.

Saris eyed her guests. "A Human and a *Tengu* dare to enter my realm together? Should I feel honoured at your visit?" She hissed in amusement, her forked tongue flicking past her fangs. Fiery red and orange spines jutted from her backbone, running the length of her body.

"*Tengu*?" Tomiko asked in apparent surprise. "Whatever is a *Ten-*?"

"Spare me your prevarication!" Saris reared herself up so that she could glare down at her visitors. "Did you seriously believe that I would not recognize a *Tengu* the instant one entered my presence?"

Tomiko grimaced, casting aside her attempted deception. "Yes, actually I did."

Saris hissed with fresh laughter. "This is the best response Sojobo could come up with? One adolescent magpie and a human infant."

"Saris, I wish to offer—" Tomiko began, but Yoshitsune interrupted her.

"Your bandits destroyed my village!" Yoshitsune snarled and drew his katana. "I have come to stop your foul schemes!"

Lyrous backed away, her own fangs bared.

Saris reared up higher and her spines rose like hackles as she hissed again. "Do not threaten me, Human!"

He brandished his katana, even as Tomiko attempted to say something. "I do not fear you."

"You will learn to!"

More curtains rippled and dozens of *Naga* emerged into the main chamber.

Yoshitsune stared at them.

Several were Pureblood, looking almost completely human in their loose shirts and pants, aside from their unblinking eyes and patches of scales. Others were Halfbloods, with far more obvious serpentine characteristics. One appeared human enough, though both of his arms ended with hissing snakes instead of hands. The twin vipers snapped at Yoshitsune.

The Pureblood *Naga* carried curved scimitars and bows.

Yoshitsune assumed a ready stance with his katana held poised to strike. "Come then," he snarled. "I will slay you one at a time or all at once!"

Saris hissed something in her own tongue.

Yoshitsune eyed her. "You will taste my blade ere I leave this world!"

"Do not fight!" another Half-Blood hissed, the words mangled by his accent almost into unintelligibility. He had the upper body of a man, but a thick snake's tail replaced his lower body and legs. He held a scimitar to Tomiko's throat. "Spill our blood and hers will join it on the ground."

"Damn you!" Yoshitsune cursed. "You fight without honour!" Nonetheless, he did not resist as two Pureblood *Naga* hastily stepped forward to seize him by his arms.

"Saris," Tomiko said, "this is wrong. We need to discuss the situation."

"Take them to a cell," Saris hissed. "They can await my pleasure."

* * *

Tomiko was escorted into a small, lantern-lit chamber by two Halfbloods—they had the bodies of men, but one had a snake's tail for legs while the other had the cowled head of a cobra. They took on positions on either side of the doorway.

Tomiko ignored them and sank gracefully onto one the red silk cushions that lay scattered on the floor. She stretched out her bare toes. *Why bother with the disguise of shoes when no one is fooled? Better to be comfortable.*

The guards watched her silently.

Is that contempt I see in your faces? Tomiko wondered. *Because I am a* Tengu, *or is it simply because I am a woman?*

A Pureblood female entered the chamber, in a delicately embroidered blue silk kimono. "Sake?" She was holding a tray. "Rice balls?"

"*Domo arigato.*" Tomiko accepted the snack with due politeness. "I grew hungry waiting in the cell." She popped a rice ball into her mouth.

The Pureblood smiled at her. "Trusting, aren't you?" she asked with a coy smile.

Tomiko smiled right back. "If Saris wants me dead, then I will be slain on the spot. Playing a trick with poison hidden in the rice wine would just insult the both of us." She lifted the small glass to her lips and drank.

"Precisely my thinking." Saris slithered into the room, a cruel smiling playing at her mouth. "Leave us." She paused until both the guards and the servant had left. "Earlier, you spoke of an offer? I trust that you were not simply attempting some pathetic ploy to save your life."

"Do you think that Sojobo would be fool enough to send 'one adolescent magpie and a human infant' venturing blindly into your lair?" Tomiko countered. "Events are gathering speed and growing ever more dark. We are not unaware of your scheming."

"And so you were sent here as spies."

Tomiko tilted her head to the left. "What manner of spy blindly enters your lair and asks for an audience with you?"

Saris hissed with laughter. "An over-confident one." She shook her head and started a sway along the length of her scaled body. "Does Sojobo have something to offer?"

Tomiko narrowed her eyes, but changed the subject. "I admit surprise that you did not kill both of us instantly."

Saris smiled. "As we have observed, the two of you are little threat to my schemes."

"Oh, I think we are *some* threat, Saris." Tomiko smiled and ate another rice ball. "You have gone to considerable trouble to hunt the two of us down."

"You are nothing," the *Naga* informed her. "The man-child, however, is another matter." Saris coiled herself on a mound of silk cushions. She positioned her head just slightly higher than Tomiko's own.

Tomiko was not bothered by Saris's posturing. "What of him?"

"The boy is dangerous."

"The same can be said of yourself."

"And of you as well, no doubt. The boy did not slay every assassin you have encountered. The body count *you* have left behind is most impressive...for one elderly woman."

Tomiko shrugged.

Saris reared up. "Let us dispense with these foolish games." Her forked tongue flicked between her lips. "You are *Tengu*. You are attuned to the mystical currents of the world. You have felt his *ki*."

"I have," she admitted. "He has an old soul."

"You can sense it...just as I can." The tip of Saris's tail twitched violently. "The boy is dangerous." Her jade green eyes flashed. "More dangerous than you realize."

"Dangerous to you or to me?"

"To us both. You cannot be blind to the meaning of his *ki*."

"So kill him then."

Saris smiled at the callousness in Tomiko's voice. "Kill *him* and allow *you* to live?"

Tomiko smiled. "I am *Tengu*, not human. What is his life to me?"

"You are *Tengu*," Saris agreed. "A race superior to the humans in every measure. As is my own." The *Naga* paused and studied her guest with a cold, unblinking stare. "Our species have known each other for many centuries."

"Yes, they have."

"We have a history that goes back far beyond the birth of the humans' so-called culture. We have no direct quarrel with you."

"Despite the assassins in Edo?"

"Some of our Human servants occasionally seek to rise above their humble station, caught up with the thrill of schemes within schemes. Accidents do happen."

"The perils of ambitious underlings."

"Indeed." Saris smiled rather sweetly. "We have given you many chances to turn away, to abandon your companion. For the respect we *Naga* share with our fellow mystics, we gave you those chances."

Her voice suddenly hardened. "You threw aside *all* of those chances at safety."

Tomiko smiled back. "We still teach our fledglings about your ancient defeat," she said and watched Saris's reaction. "The recent battle on Mount Kurama showed that we are still the superior swordsmen."

Saris hissed angrily.

"Your time is past...the world has changed."

"Changed?" Saris reared up so that her head nearly struck the ceiling. "You *Tengu* perch atop your mountains and play with swords. The humans remain cattle to be culled as we deem fit."

"That sentiment is why you lost the ancient war."

Saris brought her face down so that she looked Tomiko straight in the eyes. "The humans will suffer greatly when I return to power over them. Why should the *Tengu* suffer as well? Step aside and there will be peace between us."

"I refuse."

Saris grimaced. "You will regret this decision." She flicked her forked tongue at the *Tengu*.

"I doubt it."

"Are you safe, Tomiko?"

"Yes, Yoshitsune." She nodded to him as the cell door was locked behind her. Only a single lantern lit this tiny cell. *It is barely large enough for two of us sit down in.* "Saris only wished to question me. We had a most delightful talk, even if she chose to forego a proper tea ceremony."

Yoshitsune gestured to a tray on the floor. "We have been given refreshment. Plain water and bland rice balls. I have not touched either."

Tomiko shook her head. "Saris won't poison us out-of-hand. She'll want to kill us in some other fashion. Something painful no doubt."

Yoshitsune laughed at that. "Well, in that case...." He popped one of the rice balls into his mouth and chewed.

Tomiko sipped at the water. *The sake was much better. I should have drunk more of it.*

"We have found the Cult."

"Yes."

"We aren't dead."

"Yet." Tomiko looked around their cell. It was a small room, possibly a former storage room, with a distinct lack of furnishings other than that single lantern.

"They have taken my katana."

She heard the pain in his voice. "And they have taken my *tanto* from me. That blade is not your soul."

Yoshitsune clenched his fist. "It was a gift to me, Tomiko, and a prize beyond price. I must regain it or perish."

"Now is no time to perish."

Yoshitsune looked at her. "So what do we do now?"

"Pray...we *are* in a temple."

Yoshitsune sighed. "Tomiko, I don't want you to die."

"Trust me then. I have no plans to die here."

"Can't you *do* something?" he asked.

"Such as?" she countered.

"I don't know," he admitted after a moment. "*Tengu* are magical."

"I have limitations. I have no inherent ability to break out of this cell and overthrow a snake cult." Tomiko patted his shoulder. "At least not alone. Rest and eat. You will have need of your strength later."

"Do you think we can escape?"

"I am confident of it." She frowned as her companion sat down on the stone floor with his back against the wall. "I saw many *Naga* in the corridors and tunnels. They were all carrying crates and urns towards the surface."

"They are up to something."

Tomiko nodded. "I believe so." *Perhaps Saris is finally ready to make her move against the Shogun.* "I saw much movement. What that means is anyone's guess."

"You were not blindfolded?"

"No. No one seemed to care what I saw." She took a deep breath. "I suppose that means they expect us to be dead before we can tell anyone." *Perhaps the same reason we are locked together in one cell? Are these snakes truly* that *overconfident?* "Saris should have killed us both immediately...yet she keeps us alive."

"I will not let them harm you, Tomiko."

She smiled at him. *And how will you stop them?* she wondered as she sat down beside him.

Chapter Seventeen

Amaterasu, Goddess of the Sun, emerged from the mouth of a dark cave. She held a gleaming sword with an ivory hilt in her pale hands and now she lifted the blade high. "For the one who is worthy by the nature of his blood," the Sun Goddess intoned in a ghostly yet musical voice. "The time for battle comes again and the champions must rise to the challenge. To retreat within a cave will not save anyone." Her eyes blazed like the sun.

Tomiko opened her eyes.

The lantern was still glowing on its hook.

"How long was I asleep?" she asked sleepily. *A proper candle would have burned down and that would give me a hint as to the passing of time.*

Yoshitsune was pressed against her side, snoring softly. They were both leaning against the wall of their shared cell.

He looks so peaceful, she thought. *So very young...*

The door creaked open and revealed a large Halfblood standing in the doorway. He was mostly human in appearance, though he possessed a stubby tail as well as two normal legs. "Wake up!" he hissed.

Yoshitsune blinked and then hurriedly scrambled to his feet. "What do you want?" he demanded of the Halfblood.

The door opened further to reveal more *Naga*.

Tomiko smiled as Yoshitsune placed himself between her and the Naga. *Does he truly think that he can protect me?*

The *Naga* bared his fangs. "Come with us." His tail lashed back and forth.

The *Naga* gave Tomiko a rough push to encourage her to walk more quickly and she cried out.

"Leave her alone!" Yoshitsune ordered.

"Or you will do what?" the Halfblood hissed in amusement. He had a cobra-like hood and exceedingly sharp fangs. He glared at the human in the blue glow of the lantern hanging from the ceiling.

Yoshitsune made no answer.

They stepped into yet another cavern. Water dripped slowly from the high ceiling to splash softly into a pond.

"How many caverns are down here?" Yoshitsune asked. He peered at the murky pond. Roughly hewn stone coping surrounded it, the stone weathered and mossy.

"I have no idea," Tomiko admitted. Flecks of crystalline minerals in the rock walls and ceiling caught the glow from the beetle-lanterns and reflected it. The ceiling could still only just be seen. "It is a veritable labyrinth down here."

"Indeed, we like it this way," Saris hissed from the shadows. "Any regrets, *Tengu*?"

"I have regrets enough in my life, Saris, but none of them have anything to do with you."

Saris slithered past the pond. "I do not know what you hoped to accomplish by coming here," she said. "Alone. With neither allies nor armies." Her jade-green eyes narrowed. "You have failed."

Tomiko smiled back at her. "Your schemes are transparent," she said, pitching her voice to carry to everyone present. "Everyone knows about you, this lair, and your plans."

"If *everyone* knew," Saris hissed, "then the Shogun's samurai would be here. They are not." She turned her head towards Yoshitsune. "You cannot hope to win this war, human."

He glared back at her. "We can slay you! Sojobo told me the story of how my ancestors overthrew you and your twisted kind."

Saris's face contorted in anger, her eyes flashing. "You foolish and deluded creature!" She took a deep breath, visibly calming herself though her tail twitched violently as she continued speaking. "I have lurked here in the shadows of the underworld for centuries. I have plotted and schemed to regain all that I have lost. I am at last ready to set my plans in motion." She bared her fangs in a cruel smile. "And now one lone human child and a delusional *Tengu* think to oppose me?"

Tomiko licked her lips.

Saris stared at the polluted water in the pond. "It is a most clever trick we have played on those foolish humans. My Purebloods have been working for some time to infiltrate the city's workings. Many of the water barrels left in the streets now contain our specially-treated water."

Yoshitsune stared at the pool. The water did seem rather murky.

"It looks harmless enough, though the taste is slightly off. Assuming that the humans have taste enough to tell." She laughed, as did the other *Naga,* and flicked out her tongue. "But add a little spark and..."

One of the *Naga* struck a flint and sparks fell onto the water.

Bluish flames rose into the air.

Yoshitsune swore as a wave of dry heat washed across his face.

"Edo will burn!" The *Naga* laughed her terrible hissing laugh. "The *Meireki no Taika* will destroy the city and throw the Shogunate into chaos. In that chaos, we will strike down Tokugawa Ieyasu and all who serve him!"

"Demon-serpent!" Yoshitsune cursed. "You would slaughter thousands!"

"Yes...but they're *only* humans." The bluish firelight played off her scales. "I have been guided by the Corpse Queen...the fire is but one coil in my plan."

"You have other schemes then?"

"Of course, Tomiko."

"You surprise me, Saris." Tomiko's voice was calm, though inwardly she was shocked almost beyond belief. "I expected a mass poisoning of Edo."

"Oh, I have something similar in mind."

Now Tomiko slowly shook her head. "I would have expected something far grander," she said loudly. "'Centuries of plotting and scheming'. Isn't that what you said? Yet poisoning half a town is the best revenge that you could come up with?" Scorn was heavy in her voice. "Pathetic."

Saris hissed. "Poison is but a single aspect of the toxins we spread. Many humans will perish, yes, but the lucky ones will be *transmuted*."

Yoshitsune frowned. "Transmuted?"

"A mutation spell of some kind." Tomiko shook her head at the horrible thought now filling it. "She's going to turn her victims into *Naga* Purebloods."

Yoshitsune had turned pale in the bluish firelight. "By the Gods."

"Precisely, *Tengu*." Saris smiled with obvious pleasure as her enemies now grasped the full scope of her scheming. "What could be better revenge than turning the humans into *Naga*?" She laughed. "They should be grateful...we are elevating them into a superior species."

"They will never serve you!"

"They will have no choice."

"Sorcery." Tomiko made the word a curse. "You would twist their bodies and their minds?"

"The ritual will ensure that the *Naga* once again take their proper place as the rulers of this world. The dishonour of the past will be washed away...cleansed by a tide of human blood."

"Madness!" Yoshitsune exclaimed. "She's insane!"

As if there was any doubt, Tomiko thought. "She's had a thousand years of sulking in the dark."

"Silence!" Saris hissed. Her eyes blazed with the light of madness. "Enough talking...I have a ritual to oversee." Saris turned and began to slither away. "The Corpse Queen grows impatient for her sacrifice!" Laughing, she slithered towards one of the ramps. "Bring him to the Altar."

Tomiko nodded. *So that's why she kept us alive,* she thought.

One of the snake-headed Halfbloods cleared his throat. "What of the *Tengu*?"

Saris looked back at her servant. "She has shown that her sympathies rest with the humans. Throw her in the pond. Let the human approach his own death with her screams still ringing in his ears."

"As you wish."

The *Naga* pushed their prisoner towards the pond.

"No!" Yoshitsune struggled and one of the Purebloods stumbled. With another push from Yoshitsune, his bare foot slipped on a damp patch of stone and he fell into the burning pond with a hissing cry.

"What?" the ancient Naga demanded as she twisted around in time to see Yoshitsune drew the *tanto* from Tomiko's captor's *obi* and stab the *Naga* Halfblood with his own blade. "Stop them!" Saris screamed.

Naga hurried forward.

Tomiko snatched a rock from the ground and threw it at a cowled head. Her victim grunted and collapsed.

Yoshitsune snatched a scimitar from one of the startled *Naga* and used it to disembowel its former owner.

"Run!" Tomiko cried out.

* * *

"There they are!"

Two Purebloods raced down the ramp towards them.

Yoshitsune swung his stolen scimitar and it thudded into the Pureblood's chest. The woman fell to the ground and rolled down the ramp.

Tomiko stepped over the body without hesitation. Her toenails clicked softly on the rocky ground.

"We cannot linger here," Yoshitsune said. "Edo is in grave danger."

"We cannot flee blindly either. We need to be cautious." Tomiko hurriedly turned a corner. "This place is like a labyrinth. Every corner leads us farther away from safety."

"And never a set of stairs."

"No...the *Naga* favour these endless ramps."

They stumbled into another cavern and staggered to a stop.

A black altar dominated the far end of the cavern. Candles burned atop the obsidian stone, and the air was heavy with almost-putrid incense. Tapestries covered the walls with ornate imagery.

Tomiko cursed as she took one look. Snakes dominating human peasants. Farmers fleeing from burning huts. Blood-soaked scimitars.

Yoshitsune looked pale.

"May the Gods have mercy on its soul." Tomiko could not identify the species of the bloody sacrifice atop the obsidian stone. She glared at the statue of the hooded cobra that loomed over the altar. "A shrine to Naga Padoha," she muttered.

"The Corpse Queen." Yoshitsune stared at the skeletal snake-like face. Twin candles burned in its eye sockets. "My swords!" He snatched them from a secondary altar and hastily tied the scabbards to his waist. He stood more at ease with their recovery. "I had despaired of seeing them again."

"We still must escape from this den of serpents." Tomiko shook her head. The images on the wall tapestries were scenes of bloody slaughter by giant snakes feasting on tiny Humans. "These tunnels all look alike." She wrinkled her nose. "They all stink."

A distant bell rang with a deep rolling chime. It echoed through the tunnels.

"Saris must be calling out her troops."

"The two of us cannot hold off an army, no matter how narrow the arched doorway we might find." Yoshitsune gripped his katana. "I will not die on that altar."

"No," Tomiko agreed, "we will fight."

Yoshitsune shook his head. "You must escape." The bell tolled again and the air seemed to tremble. "Tomiko, you must go and warn the Shogun."

She looked at him. "Why would he listen to me?"

"You're *Tengu*."

"That may be of little help to our cause."

Naga burst through the cavern doorway with weapons bared.

"You are dead." Saris reared up behind her screen of *Naga* warriors. "You have cost me much time and effort, *Tengu*! Far more than your life is worth." More Purebloods and Halfbloods gathered behind her. "Take them now."

Yoshitsune threw himself at the first attackers. His katana moved smoothly in his hands as if it was alive and seeking *Naga* blood.

"Wound the boy!" Saris shrieked. "He must be alive for the ritual."

Yoshitsune sliced the head from one Pureblood and continuing the same motion, chopped the snaked-headed arm from another.

A Halfblood hissed and spat venom from his jaws.

Tomiko ducked, and then thrust a *tanto* through the Halfblood's neck. He collapsed with a harsh gurgling.

Saris screamed out something in a hissing tongue.

"We cannot hold them!" Yoshitsune cursed. "Tomiko, save yourself!"

"We go together or not at all!" Tomiko scrambled around the altar and then knocked it over, scattering the candles and the dismembered corpse, and sending Purebloods scrambling.

"Desecration!" Saris hissed.

Yoshitsune stabbed one Halfblood *Naga* and the man stumbled backwards against the skeletal snake statue.

The jaws of Naga Padoha trembled, then fell open. Viscous black liquid poured forth, splashing across the floor.

"Watch out for the venom!" Tomiko cried out. She flung her *tanto* at a snake-handed *Naga* who held a bow and was knocking an arrow.

One of the shrine's candles tipped and fell into the venom.

Blue-tinged flames erupted and spread rapidly. In an instant, the room was a hellish inferno.

Yoshitsune coughed on the sudden clouds of smoke that began to fill the cavern.

Naga screamed as the spreading flames trapped them and consumed their bodies.

Saris screamed curses.

The carved face of Naga Padoha appeared to laugh as the crackling firelight played across its features.

"We're trapped!" Yoshitsune cursed. The spreading flames had blocked the doors and were climbing the curtains and tapestries. "At least they die with us."

Tomiko coughed on the smoke.

Saris slithered towards a narrow crevice. "Damn you both!" she shrieked.

"Follow her!" Tomiko cried.

"Is there no end to this?"

"Just keep moving, Tomiko. You can do it."

Tomiko gave herself a shake. "I do not enjoy being in cramped spaces," she commented as she crawled. "This is torture."

"You're doing fine." Yoshitsune chuckled as he crawled forward. "The air is fresher at least." There was no smoke; the draft blew downwards past his face.

"We must be crawling through a ventilation shaft," Tomiko grumbled

"Saris managed it."

"She is more than half snake." *Damn this place.* Tomiko crawled. *I was born to fly, not crawl on my belly.* "I am *Tengu*, not *Naga*!" she snapped.

"Greenery!"

"What?" Tomiko gasped. "Where?"

"Ahead."

They stumbled through a screen of bushes and out of the narrow crevice and into the open air.

"The surface!" Tomiko took a deep breath and then sneezed twice. "I wish never to venture underground again. She blinked her eyes to clear them. "Ah, the stars!" They sparkled brightly overhead. "We lived through it."

Yoshitsune was looking around with dismay. "She's escaped!" he cursed.

Tomiko looked around.

They were in a clearing, near the riverbank. The darkening night was lit by the reddish glow of the burning temple.

Yoshitsune spun in place, his katana held ready. "I don't see her." He looked over his shoulder. "Where did she go?"

"She slithered faster than we could crawl." Tomiko frowned as the red glow grew brighter. "No one is trying to put out the fire." It was burning very fiercely now. *We have a struck a mighty blow then.*

"Where is she?"

Tomiko frowned. "She and her Cult will likely flee back into the shadows. She will lick her wounds and continue scheming."

Yoshitsune shook his head. "They'll head for Edo."

"How can you be certain? The *Naga* are schemers, not warriors."

Yoshitsune gestured towards the burning temple. "We're the only one who know about their plot and they must think we are dead." He himself was still uncertain of how they had escaped a fiery grave. "Saris will head to Edo and put her plan into motion. You heard her—she's been waiting for a long time. She is ready to move...and she will."

"Yes, I think you are correct." Tomiko shook her head. "Events are moving so quickly now. I am not sure that I can keep up with them."

"You will." Yoshitsune looked at the river. There were no boats along the shore, but cut ropes showed that several had recently been tied up there. "She's taken the boats!"

Tomiko nodded. "She'll make good time sailing down the Chiba. The current flows fast for this time of year." Her eyes narrowed. *Almost too fast...*

Yoshitsune snarled a foul curse. "Her damned Corpse Queen favours her with such currents! With her lead, she'll reach the city in far better time than we will. The capitol is at least a week away as a man walks."

Tomiko laughed aloud and then laughed even harder as her companion turned to stare at her. "But it's just a single night as the *Tengu* flies."

Chapter Eighteen

"There is the city!"

Tomiko adjusted her path as she soared on the night breeze.

Yoshitsune was clinging to her back as she carried him. His face was very pale and he was breathing very heavily. "Are we in time?" he called above the rushing wind.

"I hope so." Tomiko attempted to mask the exhaustion in her voice. *He sounds so nervous. I cannot allow him to feel my own fear.* "Are you doing all right?"

"Flying is for the birds!" he replied. "I am a man. I was not meant to fly."

Tomiko laughed. "I have not flown like this for far too long." She groaned as a spasm racked her chest. "Damn my age. I feel aches in muscles I had forgotten that I possessed."

"Look!" Yoshitsune gestured and almost fell from his uneasy perch. "Fires!"

Reddish glows were blazing into life below them.

"Damn! We're too late."

Tomiko landed in a dark street.

Yoshitsune slipped from her back and onto the ground. He turned and looked at her in alarm as she sank to her knees, gasping. "Tomiko?"

"I'm all right," she replied with a wheeze. "Just a bit winded." She was on her knees, gasping for breath. "I'm just not use to such exertion." *I'm getting too old to carry humans around like that.* "I should have listened to you on the road. We should have obtained horses."

Yoshitsune was not listening to her. He was staring at the city. Bright flames were already spreading rapidly through the *machiya*. Townhouse after townhouse flared with kindled fire.

Tomiko cursed. "The humans will blame this disaster on their charcoal fires, no doubt." The hissing voices of *Naga* laughed as more fires were kindled under the cover of the night. "If any of them survive."

Coarse laughter echoed from around a corner.

"We must stop them." Yoshitsune gripped the hilt of his katana.

Men were calling out now. Groups of *yoriki* normally patrolled the main streets and now they were noticing the fires and calling people to action to extinguish them.

Three cloaked men rounded the corner of the street, one of them carrying a torch, while the other two carried drawn scimitars. "Kill any who resist," one of the *Naga* Halfbloods ordered as he caught sight of Tomiko and Yoshitsune. "We leave no witnesses."

Yoshitsune drew his katana and met their charge with his own. They crossed blades

Tomiko stared at the fires as they burned. She barely noticed the three *Naga* die.

Yoshitsune shook his head as he sheathed his katana back into its scabbard. "We're too late!" he exclaimed in dismay. "The *Meireki no Taika* has begun."

Firelight was already illuminating Edo Castle.

"Then it has begun." Tomiko kept her voice steady and resolute. "We have a task still before us, Yoshitsune." She waved an arm towards the Castle. "We must stop the *Naga* from assassinating the Shogun."

Yoshitsune looked at her.

"Edo can be rebuilt, but only if the Shogunate knows order. If Saris kills Tokugawa, then there will only be chaos among the survivors."

"Chaos that she will exploit." Yoshitsune hurried down the street.

Screams had filled the air. Shouted orders to fetch water competed with the frightened neighing of horses and the gabble of fowl. The flames were spreading quickly.

Too quickly, Tomiko thought as they ran through the streets. *How did they spread so fast?* "I see fires in the Yoshiwara District."

"Most of the red-light district is burning."

"No doubt few will miss it." Tomiko tried to keep her voice light, but she could not help but wonder just how many innocents would perish this night. A thousand? A hundred thousand? "I see fires near Asakusa." She closed her eyes to blink away sudden tears. "The ancient temples are burning." The western neighbourhoods were populated with an above-average density of temples.

"The fires will be fought by the *yoriki*. They will work to save the city."

"Then we must leave them to it."

"We must hurry."

"We must walk!" Tomiko countered. "I can fly no further."

"Then we walk." Yoshitsune looked at her with concern. "Are you up to this?" he asked.

"I have come this far, I will not falter now." She took a firmer grip on her *bo*. "The *Naga* must be stopped.

"We've reached the *Takebashi*."

Tomiko nodded. "So have the *Naga*."

A dozen of the cloaked figures were trying to cross the Bamboo Bridge that arced over the moat, but armed retainers of the *Shogun* were stopping them.

"We need every hand to serve the water brigades!" one of the lesser nobles called out. "You must return to the streets."

"Stop those men!" Yoshitsune shouted to the patrol. "They started the fire! They plan to slay the *Shogun*!"

Swords were hastily drawn and many of the retainers were slain before the echoes of Yoshitsune's shout had died into silence. Several *Naga* died as well.

Yoshitsune drew his own blade and plunged into the sudden battle.

"Fool! Don't get yourself killed!" Tomiko called out as scimitars clanged against katanas.

"You must flee from Edo!"

Tomiko jumped at the voice and she broke free from the hand that suddenly gripped her arm. "Benkei!" she snapped even as her heart hammered in her chest. Her eyes blazed with anger. Her hand had drawn her *tanto* from her *obi* almost before she had realized who had accosted her.

"This is truly your final chance." The crow-headed *Tengu* gestured towards the burning city in obvious dismay. "There is fighting everywhere tonight."

"Lady Saris and her *Naga* are striking at the Shogun. This holocaust is also her handiwork."

"That snake tried to assassinate the Clan Elders as well. There is bloody battle in the mountains again tonight."

Tomiko felt a chill at his words. "What of my father?" The stench of smoke was growing heavier.

Benkei looked at her. "Sojobo lives...for now. As for the rest of our Clan...." He shook his head grimly. "We are scattered. The cherry grove is...is burning."

Tomiko shook her head. "Is she mad?"

"You must flee from the city!" Benkei told her. "There is powerful magic swirling in the air tonight. Spells and counter spells." He looked up and blinked. "I am surprised that even the humans cannot see it."

"They are preoccupied." Tomiko looked around her, taking a moment to settle her own *ki*. "You're right, Benkei." *I can feel it on the wind.* "Saris is conducting a foul ritual. She plans to corrupt the inhabitants of Edo and transform them into *Naga*."

"We thought she was just going to poison the city?"

"She's doing that and more."

Benkei looked towards the battle on the bridge. "She would twist a new breed of *Naga* into being? This cannot be allowed."

"How can she be stopped?"

"Tomiko, you must return to Mount Kurama. The Clan needs you."

"Yoshitsune needs me!"

Benkei looked back towards the battle where the swordsman was fighting with desperate skill. "He is doing all right...for a human."

"He needs me!"

"*Tomiko—*"

Yoshitsune stumbled.

"No!" Tomiko threw herself into the battle.

"Tomiko, listen to me!" Benkei hopped up and down in frustration. "Damn you!"

"The castle!"

Edo Castle was burning now. Flames wreathed one of the tall towers.

One of the samurai shook his head in disbelief as he lopped the snake-like head from the *Naga* he faced. "What happens here?"

"Demons!" someone else cried out.

"Rally!" Yoshitsune cried out. "Rally to me!" He swung his katana and lopped the arm from a *Naga* Pureblood.

More *Naga* were gathering. Many of these new arrivals were Halfbloods, led by a ferocious warrior with a snake's tail instead of legs.

"Rally to me!" Yoshitsune shouted again, seeking to hearten the shaken samurai. "For the Shogun!"

"For Tokugawa!" other voices took up the cry.

"*Banzai!*"

Yoshitsune led the samurai across the bridge in a charge.

"Slay them all!" the *Naga* leader hissed as he waved his scimitar. "Let their bodies feed the fish!"

Yoshitsune sliced through one Halfblood with his first cut, then turned to block a blow with his blade.

Men screamed as they died.

One *Naga* stumbled, clutching at his belly. He fell into the moat and blue-tinged flames erupted from the rippling water.

Men cried out in fear.

Tomiko slammed her *bo* into one Halfblood. The creature dropped to the ground.

"We're winning." Yoshitsune wasn't sure if that was truth or not, but his shaken samurai needed some strengthening.

This is not something they were trained for, Tomiko thought as she swung her *bo* at another *Naga. Creatures from legend springing out of the night to bring fire and ruin on their city? I am surprised they have fought as well as they have.* Not a single man had turned and fled from the battle.

The pile of fallen *Naga* was most impressive in the glow of the burning moat.

Samurai, those who still lived, gasped for breath.

"A victory!" one of them called out.

"Saris must have ordered every *Naga* in Japan into battle this night!" Yoshitsune took a moment to catch his breath. He gave his katana a flick to clear blood from its blade.

"Not just this battle," Tomiko told him grimly. "There is fighting in the mountains again this night."

He looked at her in horror. "Again?"

"Yes." *He does not ask how I know?* "Benkei told me...he warned me to flee from the city."

"Then perhaps you should go."

She shook her head. "My place is with you."

"Your place is with your Clan."

"I am needed here even more."

"I think we're holding." Yoshitsune glanced at his followers. They looked back at him, and several nodded to him. "We can hold the bridge."

"For now." Tomiko nodded. "But a stalemate is—"

Saris erupted from the burning moat water, her jewel-inlaid tiara glittering. "Must I oversee everything?" she hissed as flames crackled harmlessly around her scaled hide. She whipped her tail about like a whip, throwing one of the samurai against a wall with a crushed ribcage.

"Demon!" someone shouted, then screamed as an arrow claimed his life.

Tomiko looked for the archer, but one of the samurai had already spotted the *Naga* and given chase.

Saris pulled herself onto the bridge. Her body coiled there, over six hundred pounds of terrifying snake creature. She bared her fangs in a long hiss.

"Die, Demon Queen!"

Saris knocked one samurai aside and then hissed with amusement as the other humans fell back, rather than face her. "Face me then and feel the coils of death embrace you. I promise you that this night shall mark the end of the Shogunate!"

"It is your end!" Yoshitsune charged and his katana struck a glancing blow against her back. Several scales and spines fell into the moat.

Saris hissed, more in annoyance than true pain, and hastily coiled herself around the would-be *samurai*.

The katana fell from his fingers.

Her tail constricted more tightly around Yoshitsune. "I will crush the breath from your body!" she vowed. "I will offer your soul to Naga Padoha for my victory this night."

Tomiko stood staring in horror even as the rest of his samurai crossed blades with a fresh wave of Naga warriors.

"Ah, Tomiko...it is good to see you here." Saris was grinning a terrible grin. "I will feed Her your soul as well!" she hissed.

"Kill her, Tomiko!" Yoshitsune gasped.

Tomiko watched as the coils drew ever more tightly around Yoshitsune. The clatter of swords behind her told her that the desperate defence of Edo Castle continued.

"Tomiko!"

With a curse, Tomiko lunged and her *tanto* dug deep into Saris's neck.

The Naga's eyes went wide in shock. She shrieked and purplish ichors dripped from the wound, running along her scales.

"Your evil cannot be allowed to remain!" Tomiko snarled. She seized Yoshitsune's katana from where it lay on the bridge and swung the blade again and again.

Saris's head fell onto the bridge and rolled across the planks. The coil of her body loosened and Yoshitsune was released, but too close to the edge of the bridge. The coils of the dead *Naga* and Yoshitsune sank into the still-burning moat.

"No!" Tomiko plunged into the churning water after him.

A skeletal cobra loomed above Edo Castle. Smoke from scores of raging fires coiled around its face. Its jaws gaped open, revealing katana-like fangs. A forked tongue lashed out, shattering buildings.

Tomiko shook her head. Everything was hazy to her eyes and thick mist swirled around her.

"Damn you!" Saris hissed as her head floated past the startled *Tengu*. "You cannot win this time!"

The skeletal form of Naga Padoha loomed over them.

"Edo is doomed!"

A sword slashed through the skeletal snake and ancient bones exploded into clouds of dust.

Yoshitsune raised his sword again. His eyes were glowing as bright as the sun.

Saris shrieked. "*Wakamikenu no Mikoto*!"

Tomiko stared at her traveling companion as the name echoed in her ears. "The first Emperor!" His skin was burning with light, as brightly as Amaterasu the Sun Goddess herself.

Yoshitsune—or was it Wakamikenu no Mikoto?—raised his sword again. "Just as it was the last time we fought, again you and your dark Goddess are defeated and cast into the depths of Yomi." The sword glittered.

Saris wailed as the glowing sword cleaved her flat face in twain. The tiara shattered with a blinding flash of light.

Coughing, Tomiko splashed her way onto the muddy bank, dragging a spluttering Yoshitsune with her.

"Are you all right?" he asked, spitting moat water from his mouth. "At least the fires here have died. I would hate to have survived drowning to then be burned alive."

"I as well. I have never been fond of the water." She coughed, and then sank to her knees in the shallows. Her kimono hung limped on her.

"Tomiko?" He dropped his katana and knelt beside her as she coughed again, more violently this time. "Tomiko?"

She looked at him, opened her mouth, and then doubled over in pain. A golden glow washed over her body.

"Tomiko!" Yoshitsune cried out.

"Gah!" Tomiko cried out. "Ah!" She doubled over again. Her feathers fell to the muddy ground.

"Tomiko!" Yoshitsune grabbed her in his arms.

The glow slowly faded.

Tomiko was kneeling, naked, on the bank.

Yoshitsune stared at her, wide-eyed.

"What-what has happened to me?" She looked at herself in shock. Pale skin greeted her eyes and she shook her head. "Impossible." Her feet were so delicate. "This cannot be!" Luxurious black hair fell to below her waist.

"You're beautiful."

She looked at her reflection in the water.

"You're so young." Yoshitsune frowned. "You were old, with grey hair. Three hundred summers you claimed."

"*Tengu* age differently to Humans," she told him absently, still staring at her new reflection. *Some after-effect of Saris's ritual?* she wondered. "I cannot explain this."

"It's a gift from the Gods." He took her in his arms, a wide smile on his face. "They have granted you a great gift. Now we can truly be together."

She smiled back at him.

Behind them, the ash clouds hung over the city.

Discover other titles by Matt Kirkby at Smashwords.com:
Connect with Me Online:
Smashwords: http://www.smashwords.com/profile/view/MattKirkby
Facebook: http://facebook.com/MattKirkby[1]
Facebook Fan-Page: Matt Kirkby's Facebook fan page[2]

---

1. http://www.facebook.com/people/Matt-Kirkby/700512171

2. http://www.facebook.com/pages/Matt-Kirkby/176584565711824

Also by Matt Kirkby

A Novel of Lovecraftian Horror
The Death of Hope

Stories Of Feudal Japan
With Honour Veiled

Standalone
A Wyrm In the Heart
Cthonian Dragons
The Horror From The Sea
Vector Of Infection

About the Author

Born and raised in small-town Ontario, Matt Kirkby is a romantic dreamer who specializes in writing tales of high fantasy and pulp-style science fiction and space operas. He draws his inspiration from all diverse sources and ideas: Science Fiction, Fantasy, Gothic Horror, Pastoral Nature. He started his writing career submitting fan fiction for numerous Star Wars and TransFormers fanzines, but has since moved on to writing professionally. He published his first novel, A Wyrm In The Heart in 2004. He lives a double life, writing classy sci-fi and fantasy for fun under his own name, and penning gay erotica under the pen name of Frank Sol. When not writing, Matt spends his time helping his partner with his hand-crafted rocking chair business -- www.OffYourRocker.ca -- and trying to maintain some control over his cat. He still thinks that no gift is better than a new book.

www.ingramcontent.com/pod-product-compliance
Lightning Source LLC
Chambersburg PA
CBHW021212160726
47994CB00001B/447